Third Wheel

by

Kat Green

Haunts for Sale, Book 3

Third Wheel

Cover Art by *Debbie Taylor*

The Wild Rose Press, Inc.
PO Box 708
Adams Basin, NY 14410-0708
Visit us at www.thewildrosepress.com

Publishing History
First Mainstream Paranormal Edition, 2020
Trade Paperback ISBN 978-1-5092-3221-5
Digital ISBN 978-1-5092-3222-2

Haunts for Sale, Book 3
Published in the United States of America

It really was him! He was alive and well. All she could think was that at least they were together now. They could deal with anything together.

Looking up, she found the video camera in the corner, the red light telling her it was on and active. She'd almost forgotten they weren't alone. She flipped it the bird before turning back to Jonah.

"Oh, god. Hold on, I'll get you free." She went to press her lips against his, but he squeezed his eyes shut and spit in her face.

Squinching her face in disgust, she wiped at her eyes with her hands.

"What the hell did you do that for, you idiot?" she demanded. "I'm trying to help you."

"You aren't real. You aren't her," he yelled, his voice loud in the small room.

"Of course, it's me. Who else would be dumb enough to get caught while trying to save you. I'll admit, I look a bit fancier than normal in this get-up, but it was just my disguise to get in here and save you. Hold still so I can get you untied."

He began to buck wildly against the ropes holding him, making it impossible for her to cut him free. "I said STOP!"

She leaned back, sagging until she sat cross-legged on the floor and looked up at his tortured face. "What are you talking about? We have to get out of here."

With a deep sigh, he shook his head. "Neither one of us is meant to get out of here. Not alive anyway." His eyes fixated on the object on the table in front of him. "If you untie me, we'll kill each other."

She stood slowly, her own hand moving inextricably closer to the…was it another…knife?

Dedication

To Kirsten—
I will always hold a piece of you in my heart.

~

And to our ever-patient editor Lill.
Thanks for putting up with us!

Chapter 1

"Are you ready for this? I really think this house is perfect for you." Tori Jensen took a deep, steadying breath as she focused on the combination for the real-estate lock box attached to the antique patterned bronze knob. This was it. A do or die moment for a couple who had the funds and interest in claiming this as a historical home. *That's what Mildred wants*, she reminded herself.

She needed this to work. If for no other reason than to keep a promise she made to a dying woman to sell her house to the right person. There was an offer on the house from the Carolyn Miller Agency on behalf of a buyer. A good offer actually—way over the asking price—but Tori knew exactly who the offer was from and what the plans for the house entailed.

Demolition.

She knew because she used to work for the Carolyn Miller Agency until Mildred Ranier had come to her for help. Opening her own agency to compete with the horrible woman was the best decision she'd ever made. In her heart, making the sale was secondary to a greater good.

In this case, it meant she believed that houses like this needed to be saved. Unfortunately, the whole neighborhood was being bought up bit-by-bit to be torn down and made into a grandiose hotel and casino—as if

St. Louis needed another hotel or casino.

The block this house occupied was one of the two remaining holdouts. She'd passed the other blocks with pathetic pieces of paper taped to the doors showing the date they were scheduled for demolition. Each one was a sad reminder of what was at stake with this showing. Those dates were fast approaching and if she didn't get this house sold she was afraid no matter what her client wanted, this house would be added to the demo list.

Supposedly, the city only agreed to allow the casino to be built if every property was owned by the company funding the project. If any of the places didn't sell, the whole plan would be scrapped by the city planning commission. Though she doubted someone with Carolyn's connections and lack of morals would really wait for everyone to sell before knocking places down.

Still, if she could sell this house, there's a good chance it could save the whole historic community.

Tori didn't want to give up on selling the house to a family that would appreciate it, even if she knew the owner, Mildred Rainier, was sick and needed the money to pay for the medical bills piling up for her hospital care.

Mildred really should have accepted the offer from Carolyn Miller, but the woman refused to have her house sold to someone who would tear it down. And Tori knew why. She'd known from the first time she entered the house.

It was haunted.

The ghost wasn't mean—not in a scary I'm going to frighten you to death kind of way. Or at least not intentionally. He was just a little boy. She was pretty sure Mildred had known him and that was part of the reason she couldn't let the house be demolished. Where would the boy go without these walls? She needed to figure it out, and fast.

With her nerves on edge, she took a deep, hopeful breath and stepped inside the home belonging to Mildred.

The three-story Queen Anne was amazing. But it wasn't perfect by any stretch of the imagination. Besides the fact it was haunted, though she was doing her best to pretend she didn't know that, she knew the good far outweighed the bad. There were still some small areas needing attention, like the appliances were out of date and the whole house could use a fresh coat of paint but mostly it had been restored by Mildred's family money.

Money which was all gone. Spent on the pet project of a charming old woman because the house had been in their family since it was built in the 1870's when it was used as a boarding house. She'd wanted to keep it as a part of the family history to be passed on from generation to generation. But Mildred never remarried after her husband and their only child died in a skiing accident and was the last in her family line, leaving the home up for grabs.

Situated in the center of the St. Louis metropolitan area and only a short jaunt from Forest Park where the 1904 World's Fair was held, the house looked like it could have been in the musical *Meet Me In St. Louis.* She could even picture Judy Garland singing and dancing with snowmen in the front yard during the winter.

This was the first showing in weeks and she had

high hopes for this couple after they expressed an interest in living in a home that could be listed in the National Register of Historic Places. It wasn't yet, but if they filed, the house would be protected just like Mildred wanted. Being on the registry would allow the new owners to repair, but not rebuild or replace anything on the outside but make it their home inside.

It didn't, however, protect it from being torn down like Mildred thought. She'd wanted to file when she was forced to move out because of her health and took a semi-permanent residence at St. Mary's hospital but Tori had begged her to hold off. There was a chance the house wouldn't sell because of it and she would lose everything.

"I promise you," she said again, glancing over her shoulder at the couple behind her. "This house is for you."

"You keep telling us this is the perfect house," Bob McAkre said from behind her. He had his arm around his wife, Bethany's, shoulders and was tapping a finger impatiently on her arm, a smile on his lips and a twinkle in his eyes. They were adorable but, then, newlyweds looking for their first house together always were.

"Don't worry. I'm not exaggerating. You won't be disappointed," she said, as she fit the key into the lock and swung the door inward.

The hair on her arms stood up. Someone was nearby.

You promised...

The harsh whisper in her ear was the voice of a young boy. He sounded scared and angry all at once. As she paused in the entry, she heard him tap-tap-tap up the back staircase.

Swinging around, she realized the McAkres hadn't heard as they continued to smile and snuggle closer together waiting to follow her inside. This was good. They couldn't hear him. That meant the boy wasn't truly angry yet.

She wanted to yell out, "But you promised me something, too!" Last night in the foyer, she begged the spirit to be a good boy today. She'd promised him peace with a nice family if he did. Had his silence meant consent or dissent? It was too late now to find out.

Luckily, the McAkres were completely oblivious to the whirlwind of thoughts swirling through Tori's head as she eased the door the rest of the way open and stepped inside. Bob dropped his arm from Bethany's shoulder, so they were hand in hand as the couple stepped over the threshold.

"I've been too excited to eat all day," Bethany said in the breathy voice, pausing to shake her hand, "Even my students noticed how jumpy I was. From everything you've told us, Tori, I just know this is going to be our house."

Tori's hope soared. She already had the wife convinced. Now she could just work on the husband.

Bethany stood an inch or two taller than her husband. Her long blond hair and slim build gave her the willowy look of a fairy princess.

Bob strolled from the formal entrance vestibule into the main foyer like he owned the place already and Tori held her breath to hear his first reaction. As an architect and city planner, he would be the harder sell of the two. She knew he would see past the layers of hideous green and pink wallpaper to see the carvings on the railings and the intricacies of the crown molding, the question was if he would like it.

Though the room was small, the entryway was still spectacular. The stairway curved to the right then becoming a balcony on the second floor overlooking the warm wood floor beneath their feet. Above the two doorways leading into the house were carved flowers fitted with rose colored glass, that sparkled in the midafternoon sun filtering through the windows.

"I can tell you I like the woodwork already," he said, eyeing the staircase with a critical, architect's eye. "But these old houses can be deceiving. They may look good, but the question is if they're structurally sound after all these years."

Tori nodded. "You're absolutely right, but we've had the entire place examined and all the joists and footings are secure per the included home inspection. I think you'll like what you see." Squaring her shoulders and brushing her tawny hair away from her face, she pointed out the original oak woodwork on the spiraling staircase.

"As you can see this house was built in the late 1800s but while the inside has been updated, it has been preserved to keep it authentic. I know you said on the phone how you like unique, older homes. This one is even eligible to be placed on the National Register of Historic Homes if you're interested in applying. I'm proud to say I know the former owner and that is exactly what she wanted. She would have done it herself if she hadn't been hospitalized."

"Oh, no. Is she all right?" Bethany asked, placing a hand over her heart as if she actually felt sorrow for someone she hadn't met.

"She's dying. Old age. She's had ninety-nine wonderful years in this home. She'd be happy to know a couple like the two of you were living in the house."

"The floral wallpaper is a bit much," Bob said, pulling them back on topic. "Is it even wallpapered on the ceiling?"

"In some rooms, but that was the style," she explained. "Remember, wallpaper can always be removed, just as paint can always be changed. But to preserve the essence of the home, keeping everything just as is will help your investment hold its value."

"I think it adds character," Bethany cut in, walking closer to the wall, where a pink rose was at least as large as her head. "In another house it would be gaudy, but here it complements the woodwork. I'm not sure about all the pictures on the walls, though. It's kind of distracting."

Tori tried to keep the smile plastered to her face when she wanted to cringe. She loved this house as it was, but she would also love it if someone said to heck with the investment, tore down the paper and painted the entry a lively yellow or even a blue.

"I know but there's been a bit of delay with removing the owner's possessions. Seems there's no one to inherit them. But all of the woodwork is original and has been painstakingly restored. The floors, the door frames, and all the wainscoting and moldings. There's also a working fireplace in the drawing room to your right. The owner has the original shipping paperwork on the fireplace which was crafted in England and shipped here in 1873."

"I do love the detailing of the mantel and the tiling." Bethany ran a finger down the ornate wooden mantel and tiling surrounding the fireplace opening. "Bob, come and look at this. It's a seashell pattern. Almost like the one we saw at that bed and breakfast in Vermont on our honeymoon."

"You're right," Bob agreed, studying the white and blue tile. "And the fireplace is a Queen Anne, just like the house."

Tori looked away from the fireplace distracted by a movement behind Bob. Cocking her head to the side, she stared as the window slid open a tiny bit, letting in a gust of wind which sent the floor length curtains billowing inward. Her heart hammered in her chest and she blinked, hoping the couple hadn't noticed. How could she explain windows that slide *up* on their own? As nonchalantly as possible, she pushed the window down and whispered, *Stop it!*

"But, Bethany, you know we can't choose our home based on a tile we saw on our honeymoon." Bob said, laughing.

He was pragmatic. Tori wasn't sure she liked that about him, but at least he was keeping his wife distracted from what was happening by the window.

"Fine, be a party pooper but I think it's fate," Bethany shivered, wrapping her arms around herself. "It's cold in here. Wasn't that window open when we came in?"

"Why, yes. I think it was, but I closed it. I was a bit chilled too," Tori lied, sliding the lock at the top.

"What other rooms are there, Tori? I'm dying to see the kitchen," she said.

"Follow me, it's at the back of the house." She led the couple through the dining room with dark and light patterned floor and past the second drawing room with its sculpted door frame. "Here we are. The cabinets are completely…"

"Hold on," Bob put up a hand as if he was directing traffic. "I didn't see a bathroom. You said there were three."

"Yes, there are, but none on this floor. There's one in the basement the owner installed in the 1980s. There's one in the master suite and also one at the top of the back staircase, right through the door at the back of the kitchen. It used to be the maid's stairway. How fun is that?" She placed her purse and the paperwork for the house on the counter, pushing it to the back so it was up against the brick backstop. "The door is right back here."

Leading them across the room to the back corner, she placed her hand on the knob when there was a loud crash behind them.

"Oh no, your purse and all your papers," Bethany's voice was sympathetic as she rushed back to the counter and bent down to retrieve Tori's things. "I hate it when my purse spills. Bob, help me with this."

Tori stared for a moment. She knew she'd pushed her purse back to the wall, but it and all her papers were strewn over the floor. And her purse hadn't spilled. It had exploded. Her stuff wasn't just in front of the counter, it was scattered across the room.

How was she supposed to sell this place? The ghost of the little boy was working to make this place a difficult sale. How could she explain to him that if the wrong person bought it, they might remodel it or worse…have it torn down! This was prime downtown real estate after all. Casino or no casino.

Her experience with ghosts was limited. She knew

she could see them though she didn't want to and tried to avoid places ghosts tended to reside. In fact, though she'd been in this house before Mildred got sick and felt the spirit's presence, she'd never seen the ghost until Mildred went to the hospital. She was in over her head here and knew it. Luckily, it didn't appear either Bethany or Bob were sensitive.

"Oh, I'm so sorry about this," she blushed, reaching for a tampon before Bob could retrieve it for her. "I don't know what happened. I'm usually so careful. I guess I'm a little too excited about this house's potential. I really think it's the perfect place for you. One that will become a home just like it was for the several generations of Ranier's who lived here. I firmly believe a house needs to become a home because everyone needs a place where they belong. But I'm blathering on again. Please, take a look around while I clean this up."

Kneeling down in the center of the room, she began gathering the papers for the sale. They were hopelessly out of order now but that couldn't be helped. Reaching for another pile her hand stilled. An image flickered before her eyes. A young boys' face, right next to hers.

She blinked once and he was gone.

"Come on. That's not..." she glanced at Bethany and Bob. The couple had already gathered most of her stuff.

"What?" Bethany asked.

For a moment, she wanted to come clean. She wanted to tell them about the ghost and how she needed them to buy the house to keep it from being demolished. She was sure they'd already seen the papers on the other houses lining the street. She opened her mouth to tell the truth, but nothing came out. She couldn't do it. They'd never want this place if they knew about *him.*

"Oh, nothing. Just talking to myself about a…a…another thing I wanted to show you upstairs," she brushed away the incident, but found her hands shaking and the hairs on the back of her neck standing on end.

The boy was definitely here and not being good at all. Her heart was beating so hard she was sure it was pumping out of her chest like some character in a cartoon.

She was scared and she didn't know what to do. She needed help, but who did you call when you needed to sell a haunted house?

"Why don't I show you that bathroom," she suggested, standing and gesturing to the back stairs. "Did I tell you the best part? It still has the original toilet with a wall mounted tank and a pull chain."

"Does it work?" Bob asked.

"I haven't tried it myself. Let's go have a look." Placing the papers back on the counter she opened the door.

You promised.

She whipped her head around. This time the voice was louder. She even felt a painful tickle from the *ssss* sounds vibrate through her eardrum.

"Everything ok?" Bob asked, his dark brown eyes looking her over with concern. "You seem out of sorts. We can do this another day."

She didn't have another day. She needed to sell this house. To the McAkres.

"No, I'm fine. I just like the woodwork in here."

The walls were a bare white, but Bob was too much of a gentleman to point that out, though she noticed him share a concerned look with his wife. She was blowing it.

"It is cozy," Bethany said. "I like the way the stairs curve."

"Winding staircases were popular in the mid-1800s," she explained starting up. After ten steps she reached the square landing and turned to her left.

I don't like them. You said I would like them. I want Sissy.

The apparition of the little boy at the top of the staircase made Tori stumble backward. Bob caught her before she could fall.

She was exasperated and wanted to spank the petulant child. *Could you even spank a ghost?*

Of course he didn't like them. He didn't even know them yet. That's why she'd asked him to trust her which he obviously wasn't doing.

"I'm starting to worry about you," Bob said. "Are you sure you're ok?"

"I'm fine. Low blood sugar. Shouldn't have skipped breakfast this morning, I guess." She wasn't fine. She was far from it. But she needed to press on. For Mildred. "You're going to love this bathroom. It's just at the top. I can't wait to see if the…"

The push came at her knees as if the little boy had rushed at her, knocking her legs out from underneath her. Unable to keep her balance, she fell backwards, tumbling head over heels down the worn wooden stairs. Each time her body smacked into a step it felt like a taking a full swing from a baseball bat to the side. She tried to stop her momentum with her arm until she felt the bones snap. She screamed with pain as she tumbled to the bottom, landing in a heap at the couples' feet.

"Tori! Tori! Are you all right? Bob get your phone! Call for help!" Bethany was kneeling beside her.

She tried to focus on the ethereal face on the first landing, but all she could feel was the pain in her arm and a throbbing in her chest. Her vision bobbed in and out as she tried to stay awake. The pain was too much.

"I want Sissy." the boy yelled, before he disappeared into thin air.

Chapter 2

Three days later

Sloane Osborne blinked at the sudden light as she stepped off the jetway and into the crowded terminal at Lambert International Airport. Slinging her duffel bag over one shoulder, she cringed at the weight. Why was it she'd pay an arm and a leg to fly her ghost hunting equipment across the country, but she could never make herself pay to fly her clothes? It just didn't seem worth it. She just threw what she needed in an overnight duffel she could keep slung on her back.

Especially when she'd only be staying a few days. She already had a line on a house in Idaho, of all places, where there was an orb following the owners around. They wanted to sell, and she wanted the sale, as long as the pictures they'd sent weren't fake.

But for now, she was in St. Louis. A fellow real-estate agent, Tori Jensen, had called with a somewhat personal problem. The house she was trying to sell was haunted and she didn't think it could be sold with the boy in the house. She said the boy wasn't mean but had pushed her down the stairs during a showing because he didn't understand why someone new was coming into the house.

She was a sucker for an agent in need, especially one begging from a hospital bed to come check out the house and help a little boy move on. She'd hopped on the next red-eye flight to St. Louis, arriving before the sun had a chance to rise. Agents needed to help other agents and this girl was definitely underplaying a haunting where an entity pushed a living person down a flight of steps!

To avoid making contact with any of the cranky, tired people hurrying through the airport, she kept to the side, hugging the wall as she made her way to baggage claim to get her equipment. Even though it wasn't yet five in the morning, the place was full of travelers. The only thing she liked about airports was people watching.

Throngs of business travelers in their pleated suits with laptop bags slung over their shoulders hurried on their way, already on their phones as if the two-hour flight had ruined their chances at success and they were trying desperately to make up for lost time.

Families with small children banded together, mothers pushing strollers loaded with everything except their children while dads held onto the chubby hands of exuberant toddlers who'd been contained too long. There were the people rushing to catch transfers not paying attention to who they almost trampled on their way to the next terminal.

Then others with cellphones in front of their faces and headphones covering their ears walking in a daze. That's right, she thought, hide behind your electronics and don't risk the possibility of human contact. She secretly wished one of these dazed individuals would run into something, just for a giggle.

Then there were the beautiful women in the colorful saris who seemed to float instead of walk, the teenagers trying to look 'cool' with their earbuds in as they slouched behind their families pretending they were on their own, and the parades of uniformed pilots and flight attendants with their small rolling suitcases walking with the confidence of someone who'd navigated these halls dozens of times before. They acted as if they owned the place, which they kind of did.

When she reached the baggage area and hauled her equipment off the carrousel onto a waiting cart, she saw a ghost pacing beside the luggage. He wrung his hands in worry, not even looking at the people shoving each other out of their way to get to their bags.

Still spooked every time she noticed the undead wandering among the living, it was fast becoming a regular occurrence in her daily life. Most of the time, she avoided the spirits lest they realize she saw them. Cause then…all bets were off. They'd follow and harass her endlessly.

Sloane took a deep breath in through her nose and closed her eyes. She was spent and she had a terrific headache to boot. It had settled in her temples before she boarded the plane in Colorado. All she wanted was a few minutes to relax. Why was it sitting in a plane took so much energy?

She needed something to drink. Water, preferably and even though it was overpriced and undersized, she pushed her money into a vending machine, chugging the whole bottle before reaching for her change and buying another to put in her purse for later. She wanted to leave but couldn't. There was something she had to do before leaving the airport.

Parking her cart near a wall, she leaned her back

against the cool polished brick, crossing her arms over her chest as she secretly allowed her focus to turn to the ghost who'd caught her attention. He needed help.

He wore dark gray slacks and a pale blue button-down shirt. Dark brown suspenders hefted his waistline a little higher than today's fashion deemed acceptable, causing his hems to barely brush the tops of his shoes. His head was almost bald, with a short crop circling his head above his ears and wispy strands of white crossing over from right to left without concealing the age spots on top. He didn't look out of place though. He looked old. At least eighty. Possibly more.

He was all by himself, staring at the ground and mumbling something under his breath. Every now and then, he'd look up, his eyes anguished and glance around the room as if looking for someone. People passed by, ignoring him as if he wasn't there, which was mostly true…because no one besides Sloane could see him.

She waited patiently, while people retrieved their luggage piece by piece from the moving terminal. She wasn't in a hurry. The man wasn't going anywhere. It made her heart hurt wondering how long he'd been there. How long he'd had something weighing against his soul and tethering him to this plain of existence.

When the area cleared, she left her cart where it was, pushed herself away from the wall, and cautiously approached. She didn't know how he'd react, and she didn't want to scare him.

She snorted to herself. Ha! She didn't want to scare a ghost.

"Excuse me, sir?" she didn't try to touch him, she wouldn't be able to anyway, but stepped in front of him to get his attention.

The man didn't look up.

"Sir?" She tried again. "Is there anything I can help you with?"

He lifted his head, looking at her. She could see comprehension dawn when he realized she was looking at him.

"You're finally here?" he whispered. "And you can see me?"

"Yes, sir. I can see you. And I'd like to help you if I can."

The man lifted a hand to cover his face as he started to cry. She glanced around. A few people were giving her weird looks. She understood completely. It did look like she was talking to herself, after all. She shrugged. If St. Louis thought she was crazy, that was ok with her.

"I knew one day someone would come to help me!" the man exclaimed.

"I'm here now. What can I do to help you move on?"

"My Sarah doesn't know."

"Sarah? Your wife?" Sloane asked.

"No, my granddaughter. I wanted to thank her for taking care of me all summer and how sorry I was we fought just before I left. And I didn't get to tell her how much I love her. She needs to know."

"Well let's call her then," she suggested gently. "Can you tell me her last name and where she lived?"

"Farrel. Sarah Farrel. She lives in the city, near Christ's Church. She's an accountant. Always working on people's taxes."

Using the information he supplied, she did a little

research on her phone, coming up with what she suspected was the number for his granddaughter sooner than she'd expected.

"Oh, thank you. Thank you."

She dialed the number, and he waited for Sarah to answer.

"Hello?" A child's voice. Possibly the wrong number. She'd have to look harder. It wasn't like she had FBI security clearance and could find anyone she wanted. Where was Jonah when she needed him? Probably out schmoozing bad people with his boobalicious partner.

"Is Sarah there?" she asked, figuring it didn't hurt to try.

"Grandma! The phone is for you."

Buckle up, Sloane thought.

"Yes?" A woman answered.

"Hi, my name is Sloane Osborne and I have a message from your grandfather."

The phone receiver rustled on the other end of the line.

"Please don't hang up, Sarah. We are sitting at Lambert and he wants to tell you…"

But Sarah interrupted her. "I don't like practical jokesters. Do you have any idea what time it is here? If my daughter wasn't sick, I wouldn't even be up. For your information, my grandfather died of a heart attack almost twenty years ago. I'd thank you to kindly hang up and not bother me again." Her voice was crisp.

Sloane cast the man a sad look. He'd been here a long time. Not that he had any concept of time.

"I'm sorry for the timing of the call. He said you spent the summer taking care of him and he wanted to thank you." Keep it simple. This poor woman was already reliving a terrible memory. "And he wanted apologize for the fight you two had."

There was silence on the line. For a moment, she thought she'd lost her connection, but then she heard the woman take a deep breath.

"We did have a fight." Her voice broke. "After his pneumonia cleared up, he insisted on flying to Massachusetts to see his sister. I didn't think he was strong enough. Then he had a heart attack at the airport." She began to cry. "Is he really there?"

"He is. Hopefully my calling you will help him be able to move on."

"Tell him I miss him every day," Sarah whispered.

"I'll do that." They hung up. She smiled at the man, feeling the joy now surrounding him.

"Is there anything else I can help you with?" she asked him.

"No…no…thank you. Thank you from the bottom of my heart."

He rested his hand against his chest right over where his heart would be. A shaft of light appeared above him and the old man faded away, becoming one with the light.

"Goodbye, Sir," she whispered.

With a smile on her face, she headed toward the exit, intending to find a cab, but was surprised to see a lady standing by the door with a sign reading "Sloane Osborne."

The woman was wearing a dark gray two-piece jacket and skirt suit set and shiny black heels with pointed toes, she was currently tapping in an annoying rhythm. Her brown hair was pulled away from her face in a tight bun on top of her head. She looked like a lawyer from a TV show.

She made Sloane feel self-conscious because she'd neglected to dress business casual and instead opted for jeans, a comfy shirt, and running shoes for the flight. She brushed her dark hair out of her eyes and tried to smooth the wrinkles out of her shirt. She hadn't expected a pick-up, especially this early in the morning. And she really didn't want to deal with anyone until she'd had a nap, a strong cup of coffee, something to eat besides airplane pretzels, and a long soak in a hotel tub.

"You're Sloane, then?" the woman asked, stepping in front of her. "I recognize your face from your website."

"I am. Are you Tori? I'm surprised they let you out of the hospital so soon."

"I'm Carolyn Miller." The woman held out a hand with long red dagger-like nails.

Sloane glanced at her hand but didn't move to take it.

"I'm sorry, who?"

"Carolyn Miller of the Carolyn Miller Real-Estate Agency," the woman said, lowering her hand, obviously annoyed. "We are the top-selling agency in all of the greater St. Louis area."

Sloane stared at the woman, wondering if any of that was supposed to impress her.

"I'm also on the National Association of Realtors."

Ah, the NAR was something she did know about though she hadn't known this lady was on the board. Even if she didn't like her or her smart suit, she knew she had to play nice.

"It's great to meet you," Sloane said, "I'm sorry if I seem rude, but Tori didn't say anyone would be here to meet me. I was planning on taking a cab. It's rather early to get someone out of bed just to drive me to my hotel room."

Clearing her throat, Carolyn donned a forced smile. "Let me explain. I have an offer in to buy the house Tori called you about. She was a former agent at my company and branched out on her own. Being my current competition, she's launched this whole haunted house nonsense to squelch my sale. As one agent to another, how about I expedite your entire visit and bring you right to the house so we can get this whole matter settled."

"I…" she started to object when the woman took a breath, but Carolyn wasn't done talking.

"It'll be so much easier this way and we can keep it between the two of us. I don't want any more attention drawn to this place. I'm positive my buyer is about to receive an accepted offer from Ms. Ranier and just want to buy the house as quickly as possible. Do we understand each other? Besides, no one likes taking cabs these days," she said

"Well I do," Sloane cut in, annoyed since she actually enjoyed cab rides. "And I'm not sure what you're saying. Tori called me here because of a haunting. I can't just ignore it because the house will be sold. She wanted me to help the ghost move on."

Carolyn paid her no attention as she turned and headed for the exit, dragging Sloane's cart behind her as her designer heels clicked with each step on the smooth flooring, making a noise like popping gum. She wrinkled her nose in dismay but followed the woman down the line of cheap cars to the shiny Lexus on the end.

Figures she'd own a Lexus.

Without asking, Carolyn loaded Sloane's things off the cart, filling the trunk before circling around to the driver side.

She shrugged. It saved cab fare.

"I booked a room at the Chester and I've already arranged early check in," she said, sliding into the passenger seat. "I won't be able to set-up for a proper investigation until tonight, so I'd appreciate it if you'd take me there."

"That's not possible," Carolyn said, checking her lipstick in the rearview mirror before turning the key in the ignition. "My buyer needs the paperwork signed within forty-eight hours before the offer expires. I cannot believe you were even called into town for such nonsense. There's no ghost or any such ridiculousness in that house and once you walk around inside for a few minutes, you'll see that. Then I'll bring you directly back to the airport and you can be on your way to whatever sale you've put on hold because of Tori's call."

The car eased into the circle of airport traffic, heading away from the pick-up zone.

Sloane held up her hand. "Excuse me? I was called in by a terrified woman and she seemed to know what she was talking about. Don't you want to know if there's really a ghost in the house, even if just for your buyer's sake?"

"Look dear, Tori is delusional," Carolyn scoffed. "You wouldn't believe how many new agents get so nervous showing houses they do something crazy, like tripping. Stuff like that happens all the time. I'm sure she just fell and was not pushed, as she claims. I assure you, there's no ghost in the house. My clients are part of a neighborhood improvement project and Ms. Ranier's house is one of the last impediments they are facing. The whole block is slated for a tear down so either way, it doesn't matter what's inside the building. Ms. Ranier has been offered above value price but now Tori is being a pain in the ass. Truth be told, Ms. Osborne, Mildred Ranier is racking up all kinds of medical bills and needs my sale to finalize to prevent her financial ruin. Silly. It's an obvious choice for her, really. Tori is just bitter."

Sloane wrinkled her nose in disdain and didn't comment even though she wanted to scream, "LET ME OUT OF THE CAR!"

Tori hadn't sounded delusional on the phone. And in the short time she'd had to do research on the case, Sloane found out about multiple deaths in the house, a few of which were unexplained. It was a prime spot for a haunting.

"What is your plan if this is not the open and shut case you'd like it to be?" she asked.

Carolyn eased her Lexus out of the airport parking terminal, using her blinker and checking her blind spot twice before changing lanes and taking the ramp to merge onto the highway.

"It is. And all I need is a written statement signed by you stating the house is *not* haunted," Carolyn said, glancing at Sloane. "For the press in case Tori goes to the papers. The new owner is high profile and if anything came out about Tori and her delusions, he wants to be prepared. I figured since you were coming anyway, I could at least use your name. Tori Jensen is claiming the house shouldn't be sold unless the ghost in the house have been dealt with."

"Excuse me? Not haunted?" Sloane demanded. "Listen here, I'm not signing anything until I do my own thorough investigation. Unless you want *me* to go to the media that is?"

"Are you threatening me? I can't believe this. Of course you'd go to the press. People like you are only looking for their fifteen minutes of fame." Carolyn's eyes narrowed as she stared at the road ahead of her. "You won't find it here."

"People like me? What exactly do you mean by that?" Sloane demanded.

"You and your paranormal business are sullying the real-estate name. Houses are sold to become the perfect home for each buyer, not to be made into the showy fantasy world you provide."

"And yet you still want me to sign your statement," Sloane remarked, crossing her arms and leaning back in the seat.

"Somehow people seem to believe your word about haunted houses. You're the most sought-after person in that realm, though I don't understand it myself. I figured we could use your name. My buyer can't have any hint of bad press and asked me to have someone sign an affidavit stating this home is ghost-free. I'll even offer you up twenty-five percent of my commission. That way you'll get paid for your time coming out here. I'm only asking that my client is allowed to buy this home free and clear without a hint of a scandal."

"And you think, even though you've insulted me

about a hundred times since I got in the car, I'd be willing to give you that...*if* it's true. Let me investigate the place, on my own schedule with my own equipment."

"I'll write you a check for $500,000 if you walk through the house, sign the document, agree not to talk to the press, and leave tomorrow. I really don't have time for this nonsense. Haunted houses are make-believe fairy tales. I did my research on you and know all about what you did in Texas.

"And then there was the graveyard robber in one of the Carolinas and the neighbor who wasn't a neighbor in Maine. I find it interesting the type of people who rave about you online. I googled 'Help there's a crazy ghost in my house and I need to sell it now' and guess whose name popped up at the top of the page?"

Sloane took a deep breath, leaning back against the passenger headrest and closed her eyes. The woman had gone beyond mocking her and was blatantly attacking her and her way of life. Wow. That was a new one. She was honestly tempted to open the door and jump out. It might be better than listening to her. But a little voice in the back of her head heard that number again...$500,000. That was a lot of money to Sloane. Why would Carolyn really be offering her that much money? Something else was going on here.

"I didn't know my name would come up for that search," she said instead. "Cool. But if you'd really done your research, you'd know I can't be bought. Besides, if you're so sure the place isn't haunted, why rush me out of town?"

Carolyn glanced over at her, with a slight smile as she took an exit off the highway. "Once you sign the affidavit, I don't care what you do as long as you don't talk to the press. If you want, stay in St. Louis. You can have a nice vacation here in the Gateway to the West. You'll have to go to the Muny. It doesn't matter what's playing, everything is good.

"It's the oldest and largest outdoor theatre in America. All of Forest Park is worth a look. And there's also the City Gardens. They're kind of like a splash park and outdoor art exhibit all in one." The woman sounded like a recording. How many times had she used these lines as a sales pitch?

"I'm not signing anything until I've investigated the house," Sloane said. "And I'm not doing that until I've had a nap and a bath. I appreciate you coming to the airport to get me, but I'm not in the mood or the state of mind to go to the house right now. Please take me to the Chester. If you insist on taking me to the house right now, I'll just call a cab from there making this process that much longer."

Pulling the over-priced airport water out of her purse she twisted it open took a drink as she tried to ignore Carolyn's snort of disdain staring out the window and watching the houses pass by, their windows glinting off the still lit streetlamps.

The sky was just beginning to lighten as the sun rounded the horizon but there were signs of people waking—lights in windows, joggers with dogs and even a few early morning commuters climbing into their cars. This was a nice area. Lots of big houses. It didn't look like any city she'd been in before.

"Where are the tall buildings? I thought this was a city?" she asked, trying to change the subject and get Carolyn to stop grinding her teeth. The sound was annoying and gross all at once.

"Oh, it is," Carolyn replied. "But I always think of it as a city with charm. The big buildings are down by the river, where the arch is. The rest of it could be mistaken for a suburb, but it's all St. Louis."

She eased the car to a stop in front of an elegant Tudor style building with whitewashed walls cross sectioned with dark brown wooden beams. It looked like a tavern straight out of Medieval England, even down to the wooden guild sign with a rampant lion.

"Here we are. I can't believe *you* are staying at The Chester. It's one of the best hotels in the city. How do you afford it?"

Should she tell her how selling haunted houses was becoming profitable? She wasn't rich but she had enough. She doubted the woman would appreciate the comment. Instead, she got out of the car to unload her bags.

Carolyn followed.

"I took the liberty of typing up a statement for you. All it needs is your signature and I can proceed with my sale." She slid a slim manila folder into the outside pocket of Sloane's duffle.

"And the seal of a notary," Sloane put in.

"Which I am. No worries there."

"Not going to happen. I'm investigating that house before I sign anything."

"I demand to be with you when you walk through the house," Carolyn spat. "You will sign this. Or else."

"Or else what?" she asked, completely perplexed by the animosity coming from the woman. Could she really hate her because she was a paranormal real estate agent or was there something else about her that rattled the woman?

Maybe it was her ratty sweatshirt and startling good looks?

Carolyn got so close to her she could smell the stale coffee on her breath. "Look here, missy. You will sign the document. I tried to be civil, but you obviously don't know the meaning of the word. I didn't want it to come to this but since I'm on the National Real Estate Association's board, I know for a *fact* you did not renew your license this year. A real-estate license must be renewed annually. Since you've sold houses since yours expired, you are in violation. I will have your license revoked."

"What are you talking about?" Sloane demanded.

"Don't you check your mail? You would have been notified about this."

She didn't check her mail. She was rarely home long enough to sleep in her own bed, let alone to go to the post office to open her PO box. She did almost everything online anyway.

"Unless you sign this statement, I'll ruin you. You'll be done scamming people with your talk about haunted houses. You can kiss your past success goodbye, which wouldn't be the worst thing since you are an embarrassment to real agents everywhere. You'll go in front of the realtor's board and be charged with negligence and no one will hire you again."

Carolyn leaned back, giving Sloane room to breathe as she smiled tightly. "But if you say it's not haunted, this whole thing gets brushed under the carpet and you walk away a much richer woman. I'd say you have about five hundred thousand reasons to sign this document. You following?"

Sloane didn't respond. She couldn't. Instead she began loading her equipment back into the Lexus' trunk before climbing back into the car and desperately gulping down the rest of her bottle of water, wishing she had more. She was suddenly parched, and her headache was trying to pound through her skull. "Fine, Carolyn. Let's see this house right now."

She was being blackmailed.

Chapter 3

"A quick walk-through," Carolyn's tone had completely changed since she coerced Sloane to head straight for the home in question. She reminded Sloane of a spoiled toddler who was used to getting her way. It was almost like, in her convoluted mind, the crazy woman thought they were friends now. "And then you'll be back at your hotel and soaking in the tub like you want."

The "this-place-is-perfect-for-you" realtor smile plastered on Carolyn's face made her want to puke. Raising an eyebrow, Sloane kept quiet and shoved her hands in the pockets of her jeans suppressing her brewing anger. The pit of rage in her chest was threatening to boil over.

The gall of this woman! Deciding to remain civil, she worked on developing an action plan. Whether this home was haunted or not may not be evident in a quick walk-through. She needed to be ready for an argument if she needed more time to observe any paranormal activity.

"So you've never had anything happen to you that you can't explain?" she asked.

Walking briskly to the front door, Carolyn answered tersely, "Only this, Ms. Osborne."

Peeking over Carolyn's shoulder she almost burst out laughing when Carolyn entered in the code for the lock box—3-6-6-6. What else would you use on a haunted house?

"Are you sure you've never had anything happen in your life you can't explain?" Sloane pried. "A sense of being watched when no one was there? A feeling about doing or not doing something even though you didn't know why?"

Carolyn grimaced and shrugged her shoulders. "I told you before, I don't believe in ghosts or anything else that makes things go bump in the night if that's what you are asking."

Let it go. Some people were simply prejudiced against the existence of ghosts and she didn't stand a chance of proving anything to a woman who refused to listen.

Studying the home's dark green exterior which sported a wraparound front porch that hugged a turreted tower at the corner, she felt nothing out of the ordinary. The Queen Anne style was beautiful with its steeply pitched roof with a variety of gables and dormers. Haunted or not, that remained to be seen.

Part of her wanted the house to be clean so she could walk through it, sign the paper and get away from Carolyn. It was a lot of money the woman was offering for just her signature. The other part of her would be happy to see a spirit inside the walls, even if it wasn't the witching hour when ghosts tended to be the most visible.

She kind of wanted to watch as hoity-toity Carolyn Miller learned what it was like to jump out of her skin. Sloane wasn't usually this vindictive (unless she was forced to deal with Christa—her would be boyfriend's irritatingly gorgeous FBI partner) but since this real estate agent was both blackmailing and insulting her chosen profession, she would make an exception.

After entering in the digits, Carolyn retrieved the key and pushed open the front door.

"Wow, just wow," Sloane caught her breath, looking inside at the slightly curved staircase with each baluster and newel post lining the handrail intricately carved to look like vines. The wallpaper was gaudy but fit with the time period when the house would have been built. Even above the doors, stained glass was fitted into woodwork, showing brilliant outdoor scenes.

"What?" Carolyn turned back to Sloane.

She couldn't help but be impressed. The place was beautiful. Meticulously restored to be period correct and maintained through the years.

"Who lived here?" she pushed past Carolyn and into the entry. "This place is gorgeous. Why would anyone want to tear it down?"

A large crash came from upstairs and they both looked at the ceiling. She tried to hide the smirk she knew was forming on her face by scratching an imaginary itch on her nose.

"I already told you—prime real estate. Location is everything. And, by the way, that," Carolyn pointed up, gesturing vaguely toward the ceiling, "was nothing. Old houses *all* have creaks and moans, which does not mean a residence is haunted."

"I think you should let me be the judge of that," Sloane replied, shaking her head at the woman's stubbornness.

Carolyn led her into the sitting room and spread her arms out and twirled in a circle. "See, just a pretty old house. Nothing strange or unusual happening."

All at once, a picture on the wall crashed to the floor. Sloane took a step back as the glass scattered across the hardwood floor, sliding toward her tennis shoes. Being careful to avoid the glass. She picked up the frame, examining the black and white photo of a young girl resting her hand on a pudgy boy in front of her.

The girl was maybe twelve and the boy couldn't have been more than three. She wore a long dress, the collar buttoned up to the base of her chin while he sported a knickered suit and tall dark socks. Both of their faces were serious, common in early photographs. Something about the picture touched Sloane. She could feel the love and protectiveness flowing from the girl into the boy who must have been her brother.

"Do things often fall off the walls on their own?" Sloane asked, smirking as she handed the frame to Carolyn.

"Just a nail on its last threads." Carolyn insisted, though her hand was shaking when she placed the photo in a drawer and retrieved a broom to sweep up the glass. "I don't even know why it's still there. If I were in charge of the sale of this house, I would have made sure the house was empty before showing it."

"Uh-huh," Sloane muttered, taking a few deep breaths, centering herself and opening herself up to the energy in the house. By letting down her ever-present walls, she allowed the ebb and flow of all energy to pass through her and her consciousness explored the area though she remained cemented in the same spot.

With a deep inhalation, she asked for any spirits to make their presence known. When she let out her breath, she could feel it. Above her. Upstairs. "I need to go to the stairs in the back." *Oh yeah, there was definitely something up with this place.*

She didn't wait for approval, heading deeper into the house. Carolyn *click-clacked* after her until Sloane found the back staircase in the kitchen. "Are these the stairs Tori fell down?"

"Yes, but I don't see why…"

A sudden clunk-clunk-clunk had Carolyn stopping midsentence. A small red rubber ball bounced down the stairs, landing on each step on the way down. It rolled to a stop at Sloane's feet.

Sloane could tell by the way she covered her face with one hand, Carolyn was trying to hide her shocked expression. Sloane bent down the picked up the ball and tossed it back up the stairs.

A few moments later, the ball came clunking back down.

"Do you want to play?" Sloane asked.

Tossing the ball up the stairs again, a peal of boyish laughter echoed from upstairs as footsteps ran down a hall over their heads.

Sissy? Is that you?

There was no way she would agree to sign anything saying the house wasn't haunted at this point. But the bigger questions, was if this haunting was innocent or not…

"Ok, I've had enough," Carolyn exclaimed. "I don't know how you're doing this, but you must be some kind of charlatan. This is sabotage." Carolyn grabbed her arm pulling her back toward the door, her eyes wide and her fingernails digging into her arm. She was acting more like a teenager at a scary movie than a real-estate agent. "We can go now."

Sloane shook her head and laughed. Carolyn didn't want to admit it, but she was scared. Whatever was in this house was getting to her.

"You can feel it, hear it, and saw the picture fall and the ball come down the stairs. Just say it; you are uneasy in this house, aren't you?"

Releasing her arm, Carolyn brushed her off. "Most certainly, I am not. I'm a busy woman and the sooner I can get back to the office and close this deal, the better. I still need to finalize with the construction crew and meet with the bank about a bar around the block. I don't have time for your shenanigans."

"I'm going upstairs." Sloane felt drawn to the staircase, remembering the terrified call from Tori.

"You have five minutes. I'll clean up that glass." Carolyn went to the kitchen and retrieved a broom to sweep up the glass.

"If you are getting scared, put my bags on the front porch. I'd love to stay," Sloane called over her shoulder while heading up the staircase. From the corner of her eye, she caught the backside of the flickering image of a small child running up the stairs. She followed him and he turned, sitting at the top of the stairs giving her a friendly wave.

"Hello?" Sloane said, walking up a few more steps until they were at the same head height.

"*Hello. I like you,*" the boy said. "*I don't like her. Where's Sissy?*"

"I don't like her either," Sloane whispered. "Who are you?"

Instead of answering, the spirit cocked his head to the side, a mischievous light glinting in his eyes as he disappeared.

Darn. She thought she was getting somewhere.

Before she could hunt down the little boy, Carolyn let out an ear-piercing scream.

Rushing downstairs, she found Carolyn frozen in terror as the front door slammed shut then slowly opened on its own. Across from the stairs in the small parlor with an ornate tiled fireplace, the window started rising to the top, and then sinking down again over and over, faster each time.

The boy appeared in front of Carolyn. He stood on his toes trying to be taller, though he didn't even reach her waist. From the way she stared above his head at the maelstrom of activity, Sloane knew she couldn't see him.

"*GET OUT!*" the boy screamed, disappearing again. As soon as he was gone, all the activity ceased.

Carolyn flinched. Sloane didn't know if she'd heard what he'd said or felt the anger behind his words, but she felt something.

"Still saying it's not haunted?" Sloane crossed her arms over her chest, leaning against the post at the bottom of the stairs. This time she didn't even try to hide her smile. This place was definitely haunted, and the sassy little boy had his own idea of what he wanted going on in *his* house.

"No…no…nothing of the sort," Carolyn stammered, her eyes wide and her skin a shade short of ghost-like. "It's just…a…ah…a faulty window. And the wind must have caught the door. That's all."

She nodded like she agreed, trying not to laugh at the way Carolyn was trying to explain away the paranormal activity occurring right in front of her face.

"I'm just glad my buyer is planning to tear it down,

so they don't have to deal with certain…aspects of the house."

"I disagree. Tearing down this house would be a horrible idea. You'd be sacrificing the spirits living here and it would make them angry. What do you think they're going to do when you tear down their home? Disappear into oblivion? I hate to be the one to break it to you, but it doesn't work that way."

"Then what way does it work?" Carolyn demanded.

"Ghosts are tied to the location, not the house itself. If you tear down a building, the ghost will continue to haunt whatever is built on the land. And it would be stuck here, possibly without a chance to move on. You think that little tantrum was bad? Wait until you see a spirit who's lost everything they held dear. Now, keeping that in mind, will you agree to let me do a full investigation and clearing now?"

With a sour look on her face, Carolyn grabbed her purse and ran out the front door. She dropped her keys three times before reaching her car. Sloane followed, taking the time to lock the door and replace the key in the lock box. The sun was just visible now, giving the area a clean, fresh burst of light.

Two women, each holding a toddler's hand, approached Carolyn who stood fumbling with her keys, trying to push the correct button on the fob.

"Ms. Miller? Is that you?" one of the women asked, rushing forward.

As they came closer, Sloane realized the girls were unmistakably twins, both with a slim build, olive complexions and light brown hair.

"I'm sorry, I really don't have time right now,"

Carolyn yanked open the door as if desperate to get inside.

"We own the bar around the corner. The one you've been trying to buy, and just so you know, we're not budging. There's no way we'd ever sell to you. St. Louis doesn't need another casino or a hotel."

"Not in our neighborhood," her twin added moving into the street. "We've collected over one hundred signatures from people in the neighborhood who don't want that kind of business ruining the historic quality of the area."

"We'll see what the banks say when your mortgage comes due. I know exactly who you are and how much you owe." Carolyn slammed the car door in her face and the girl stepped back, her brow furrowing and her mouth turning down into a heavy frown.

"Sorry about her," Sloane said, approaching the other side of the vehicle. "Ms. Miller is slowly realizing the historical richness of some of these properties. I'll see what I can do to change her mind." Giving the girls a quick wave, she climbed into the passenger seat. Carolyn sat in the driver's seat panting, her hand over her heart and her chest heaving.

"Now then, I'd appreciate it if you'd take me to my hotel. I can start a full investigation of this house tomorrow."

Carolyn didn't answer, but she did manage to turn the key, shift the car into drive, and floor it away from her first haunted house.

****

After checking into her room at the Chester, Sloane used a complimentary cart to wheel her equipment to her room. The room was huge and decorated with dark wooden furniture covered in plush maroon and cream-colored fabrics. In fact, it was so big, she pulled the cart in, leaving the boxes filled with ghost hunting paraphernalia where they were as she kicked off her shoes and sprawled onto the king size bed.

The room was nicer than her apartment. She'd opted for a royal room because it had a bathtub. The rest of the amenities weren't as important but right now she wanted a soak with the fancy soaps the hotel supplied. She had time. Carolyn had agreed to let her look into clearing the house. Actually, she'd said "fine, clear it or whatever nonsense you do so I can sell it and tear the wretched place down."

Over her bath, she'd ponder how to convince the home's naughty little resident to move on. The pointed finger from Carolyn and "Or else" comment at the end of their interaction held that veiled threat of imposing some kind of fee or suspension on her real estate license. And that would royally suck and be visible for the whole world to see. And judge.

Sighing, she draped one arm over her eyes, so her forearm blocked the afternoon sun streaming through the large double window. She really needed to remember to check her snail mail. If she had, this would not be happening.

Needing to hear a friendly voice she pulled her cell phone from her back pocket and scrolled through her contacts until she found the info for her best-friend and probably the love of her life if they were ever in the same place for long enough…Jonah Prescott.

For a moment she stared at the picture of him she used as his screen shot. He was altogether too handsome for his own good. Or hers. His dark hair fell over one brown eye and she'd caught him with a half-smile, his mouth full of something, probably the burger he held in his hand. The man was always eating so it didn't seem fair he had rock hard muscles and she could count the pop tabs on his abs. He looked sheepishly adorable and it was no wonder she'd fallen for him…hard.

She hadn't thought love was an option after her fiancé, Michael died, but Jonah had proved her wrong. Too bad he lived near his work in Washington D.C. while she flitted around the world, to wherever someone wanted her expertise.

She pressed the call button, desperately hoping he was able to answer but her luck wasn't strong today.

Straight to voicemail.

It figures. He'd been AWOL since Maine. That was almost four months ago but he was deep undercover or something with his FBI job. Stuff she couldn't know about.

Tossing the phone on the bed, Sloane rummaged through her bag until she found the meds she'd needed since before the plane landed. She popped two extra-strength acetaminophens for her headache and gulped a bottle of water trying to figure out exactly how she'd forgotten to renew her license? She loved her job. It was important. Her reputation was all she had. She sold houses, some haunted…a place for people, living or dead, to belong.

The one thing missing in her own life.

She belonged nowhere, living like a gypsy traveling from place to place and on the road so much, even when she managed to spend time in her meager apartment, it never felt like home.

But there wasn't much she could do about that right now. She might as well try to relax and buckle up and center herself for tonight's investigation.

Sliding off the bed, she headed to the luxury bathroom. The walls were a deep red, the floor tiled in tan with mirrors lining the walls. The walk-in shower had three massaging heads, but she wasn't interested in them right now. Instead she headed straight to the free-standing white porcelain tub in the center of the room.

She placed her cell on the toilet seat in case Jonah returned her call while running warm water in the tub and adding the complimentary peach-scented bubble bath. Once the tub was half full, she performed an obligatory one-toe-in-check to make sure she wasn't stepping into scalding hot water, then slid into the tub and rested her head on the fuzzy blow-up pillow suction cupped to the back of the tub.

Since the selling haunted houses biz had become slightly more lucrative and clients footed her hotels bills, she'd come to the realization fancy hotels were *not* overrated. They were amazing.

Ever since she'd almost died of dehydration (thanks to a serial killer in Wisconsin) water had become a necessity in her life. Here, surrounded by water and feeling safe and secure she was able to relax.

Her thoughts drifted back to her transitory lifestyle. Maybe she needed to ground herself and settle into a community like Stephanie, Jonah's super-psychic aunt who lived in New York. At least then she might have more of a chance to check her snail mail if it came right to her house and not a PO Box. Then she'd know if something important was happening, like her license expiring!

Or maybe she could just get a cat. Cats could travel, right?

As her eyelids were drooping and her thoughts were drifting to places of peace, her phone buzzed and she lunged for it, hoping it was Jonah.

It wasn't, but it came as no surprise that while she was thinking about Jonah's Aunt Steph, it would be the scary old-lady herself interrupting her bath time.

Sliding back down in the tub, she toweled off one hand and pressed the button to answer the phone. "Hi, Steph. How are you?"

"You sound relaxed. What are you doing?"

Sloane let out an audible sigh. "I'm taking a bubble bath in a fancy hotel in St. Louis where some real estate agent is trying to both bribe and blackmail me into saying a home isn't haunted even though it totally is. Nice, huh?"

"Interesting. It may have something to do with my dream I had when I dozed off with my cat on my lap today. I called because I had a very vivid dream that you were going to be contacted by someone you deem untrustworthy, but for the sake of someone you love, you must trust them."

"Wait, what?"

"I can't talk right now, dear. There's a huge meeting with the assembly tonight, but I wanted to get this message to you first."

Jonah's aunt lived in the spiritualist community of Lily Dale, where you had to be approved to buy a house. Basically, *verified* psychics only. It was on her list of places to visit when she found a free moment, especially with Aunt Stephanie as her guide.

"I'll try to trust this Carolyn, but honestly, she's a

bit of a be-otch."

"Maybe it's Carolyn. Maybe it's someone else. Can't say for sure. Have to go, dearie." She made a kissing sound and was gone.

Before she could even settle back in the bubbles, there was a knock on the hotel door.

Deciding she was far too comfortable to get out of the tub, she closed her eyes and ignored the knocking. For a moment it stopped, and she felt herself relaxing with relief. Whoever it was had gone away. But after a few moments, the knocking turned into a pounding.

Someone was really trying to get her attention.

"I'm in the tub," Sloane yelled. "You have the wrong room. I didn't order anything."

She heard a key in the lock and the hotel door squeaked opened. "Hey!" she shouted, panic setting in. Her heart thumped in her chest but before she could jump out of the tub and find a weapon, the bathroom door opened to reveal Jonah's partner, Christa McBride *aka Boobalicious*.

"What the hell, Christa?" she sank into the bathtub, hoping the bubbles covered her privates, though she crossed her arms over her chest just in case. "How did you get in here?"

More importantly, *why* was she here? She was supposed to be acting as Jonah's pseudo-wife on some stupid secret mission she couldn't know about.

Somehow, she looked even more awesome than she remembered. Her long blonde hair curled at the ends, stylishly swept back off her face with a black clip. She wore painted on jeans that showcased her model-esque body. And her signature low-cut black shirt, showing off her huge knockers.

"FBI, remember? Get dressed," Christa said. "We have to go. How can you be taking a bath at a time like this?" She pulled a towel off the rack and held it open like a mother does for child after a bath.

Who did this broad think she was? Marching into someone's hotel room and into the bathroom…and, and…she was so angry she wanted to jump up and punch her in the freaking face.

"Get. Out. NOW!" she yelled.

Christa opened her hands and dropped the fluffy white towel to the floor.

"I don't see what your problem is, we all have the same parts," she openly stared at Sloane in the tub. "And I can see why Jonah is stuck on you. Been working out?"

Sloane crossed her arms over her chest and glared, though she doubted she looked intimidating, considering she was stark naked.

"Get over it and focus on what's important. Jonah's missing. I thought you'd *know*," she made quote marks with her fingers. "With your psychic connection and all. C'mon sugar, I need your help before it's too late. Please hurry." She turned to leave.

"Wait! What do you mean?" Sloane demanded, sitting up in the tub. "How can Jonah be missing? He's your partner?"

"I'll explain when you're dressed but this is urgent so chop, chop!" She barked while snapping her fingers as she sailed out of the bathroom.

"My clothes are out…"

The door opened again, and her duffel flew in, landing with a thump on the tiled floor.

****

45

With her skin not as prune-like as she would have liked, Sloane toweled off and rushed to get dressed. As promised, Christa was waiting for her in the comfy looking cream-colored lounge chair, remote in hand and flipping through the channels on the widescreen television on the wall.

To say she hated Christa wasn't an exaggeration though her reasons were so petty she tried to ignore them most of the time. The girl was beautiful, in a busty blonde barbie type of way and spent way more time with Jonah than she liked. The few times the three of them were in the same place at the same time, she felt like the unwanted third wheel. Right now, she needed to get past that. Jonah was more important.

"Now what's going on? How can Jonah be missing?" she demanded, grabbing the remote from Christa's hand and flipping off the tv.

"Have you heard from Jonah?" Christa asked, with surprise and something like hope in her expression.

"No, I haven't. He's on a super-secret case he can't tell me about." Not like she'd offer up any information to the double-D toting hoe bag anyway. Wait, she was trying to get past her dislike for Jonah's sake. *Focus.* "You're his partner. Isn't he supposed to be with you?"

"Jonah and I were working on a case together, deep undercover. I was posing as an elite antique collector and Jonah was my husband, an expert in identifying paranormal items. He would verify items I wanted to buy before we spent our money on them. Our case led us to the International Paranormal Conference in Las Vegas."

Christa explained, moving from the lounge chair to the mirror over the dresser and examining her lipstick in her reflection. "Jonah had a meeting set-up with a conference attendee they call Mr. X. He went alone, with some sort of golden Egyptian statue he was trying to trade for a cursed knife. Something must have gone wrong at the meeting. I haven't seen him since."

"As his partner, why weren't you there as backup?" she demanded, hands on hips as she watched Christa primp. Petty thoughts or not, this girl really rubbed her the wrong way. Still, Stephanie had told her to trust someone she wouldn't usually find trustworthy. Christa definitely applied.

"I wanted to be, but I had a meeting with a known criminal we've been trying to nail down for years. I told Jonah to wait for me, but he insisted we could both handle things on our own. You know how stubborn he is."

She knew all too well. The man drove her crazy. Mostly in a good way, but he did have his moments.

"The problem is Mr. X is deeply involved in the freaky paranormal thing which isn't my strength. That's where you come in. Tomorrow night, there's the banquet part of the conference and I need someone to keep this Mr. X. busy so I can do some recon in his room and find out what happened to Jonah. She paused.

"Our flight leaves in a few hours. Jonah was going to ask you to come and assist us on this case once we got to Vegas, but he didn't want you in any danger. He said you were more important to him than double cheeseburgers or something ridiculous."

Her heart swelled. That was high praise coming from the connoisseur of fast food sandwiches. "I have to make a stop on the way to the airport first. A loose end here in St. Louis."

"Fine but get moving."

****

Sloane felt funny sitting in a car next to Boobalicious. Maybe it was time to grow up and call her Christa. If Jonah really was in danger and needed her help, the least she could do was show his partner a shred of respect. Getting into the FBI must be somewhat difficult so she figured Christa couldn't be all hot air between her ears.

With a sigh, she decided she needed to start over. It wasn't Christa's fault Jonah had brought his partner to Michael's funeral. It was his, so she should let it go and be nice, even though every ounce of her being, fought the urge to tell the one about the blonde, brunette, and redhead who got stranded on a desert island.

"Here it is."

Christa slowed in front of the house and parked.

Sloane punched in the digits for the lock box and crept inside. She set up her equipment where she most expected to see activity and synced it with her phone so she could monitor the recordings wherever she was. Back in the car, she called Carolyn and left a message. "Hi, this is Sloane. Something of an emergency has come up. I need to leave town for a few days, but I'll be back to do a thorough investigation. Please…*please* don't sell the house before I get back. I'm gathering some video evidence and then I'll cleanse the place when I return. Promise."

If….*if* she could clear the house.

A text came into her phone a few minutes later.

You have 48 hours before I go to the board about your expired license. To avoid potential fines and hearings, I only need a signature. Sign and I transfer the money into your account. Your choice.

It wasn't long enough but she would have to make it work. She set a timer on her phone, counting down from forty-eight. The clock was ticking. She had to save Jonah and her reputation.

Chapter 4

After attempting to catnap on the three-and-a-half-hour flight, Sloane found herself standing on the Strip in Las Vegas, Nevada and it was a sensory overload times ten.

There were noises everywhere—cars honking, people yelling, open air slot machines zinging, even the air hummed as if the street itself had its own theme song. The neon lights lining the hotels lit the whole street like a magic carnival in the middle of the desert. And it was the desert. The dry heat hit her the minute she stepped out of the airport taking her breath away and warming her skin to the point of a burn.

She loved it.

Drinking in the sights on the cab ride to the Strip, she couldn't believe the size of the hotels. They were like cities themselves. Or civilizations, she thought, considering you could go from Ancient Egypt in the Luxor's pyramid, to Medieval England at the Excalibur, sail the high seas with pirates, or take a trip to modern Paris, New York, and Venice all before coming to the monstrosity near the end of the Strip where the cab pulled into the portico to drop them off.

The Hotel X-cellence was one of the newest additions to the line of luxury casinos/hotels but had already gained a reputation for being an upscale experience.

The blue glass building rose at least forty stories above her and was like a compound, with smaller outcroppings spreading across an entire Vegas block at the end of the Strip. The place was not only a hotel and casino but a convention center, a resort complex for the well-to-do, and a shopping mall. She even saw signs for a golf course extending behind the massive complex. It was a vacationer's dream. And probably made more money in a day than half the population of Nevada put together did in a year.

"Hey, Ozzy, are you coming?" Christa called from where she stood in front of the double sliding glass doors. "We don't have all day."

"All right, already," Sloane grumbled. "And don't call me Ozzy or I'll call you Booby." She hefted her carry-on over her shoulder and followed Christa with her designer handbag into the icily air-conditioned vestibule.

Immediately goosebumps rose on her arms from the cold. It was like taking an ice bath after sitting out in the sun. She shivered, wishing she'd packed a jacket in her bag. But how was she to know? Outside it was about a hundred degrees while inside it felt like thirty. Ok, maybe forty-five.

If Vegas knew one thing, it was opulence. The corridor before her leading to the lobby was a picture of wealth and beauty. Windows lined the outer walls letting in the sunlight to make the crystal chandeliers and wall sconces sparkle and shine. The inner walls were a bright, pristine white, like an untouched canvas. She looked, but she couldn't find one fingerprint or smudge on the glass or the wall.

Banners hanging from the ceiling announced

upcoming events. Some advertised musical groups performing on the main stage, but most were about the paranormal convention going on and the speakers appearing there.

She especially liked the one of the famous ghost hunter, Jack Sackins. Not only was he an expert in the paranormal field, his swept back blonde hair and baby blues made him easy on the eyes.

Even though it was barely noon, she could hear the dinging of the slot machines in the casino as they approached the lobby. The noise was monotonous and a little annoying, but she guessed she'd have to get used to it. After all, casinos were the way of life in Las Vegas.

Christa headed directly to the only male at the long check-in counter when they reached the lobby, ignoring the string of females working at the desk.

"We'd like to check in, please," Christa said, leaning on the counter so her chestal endowments were pressed together and bulging. Sloane had to look away. The girl was so obvious and yet it obviously worked.

While Christa was busy, she opened the app on her phone to check the monitors she'd left in the house in St. Louis, but nothing had changed. She hadn't really expected anything, but the clock was ticking.

Drifting over to the schedule for the paranormal convention, she looked over the events for the day. There was a tour of haunted Vegas, a masquerade ball that night, and even a presentation on the resurgence of an old bootleg video showing real people dying in horrific ways. She scowled. She didn't like videos showing people as they appeared after death. It was morbid and gross and didn't have anything to do with paranormal activity. She also was a little leery about how the directors got the footage. Who intentionally filmed carnage and horror?

As she scanned the rest of the list, her eyes stopped on a question and answer panel. She read the names twice before scooting back across the lobby to where Christa was getting their keys.

"Hey, Christa?" she asked.

"Hang on, honey. I'm almost done. We can talk in a minute."

Sloane kept her mouth shut until she and Christa were alone in the elevator heading to the thirty-eighth floor but then she had to have an answer.

"Christa why is my name hand-written in as being a part of the expert panel for tonight?" she demanded. "Jack Sackins is on that list! I shouldn't be there."

Christa glanced at Sloane, her brow furrowing in confusion.

"I told you I brought you out here to help. I offered your services. Besides, not just anybody can come to this hoity-toity ghost crazy get together. I'm told it's the premier paranormal convention in the country—for people who believe in that kind of thing. The masquerade tonight costs two hundred bucks a person to attend but even though it was sold out, I managed to score us tickets."

"How?"

"It's part of what I demanded when I said you'd appear on the expert panel at the 11th hour."

"But I have no idea what I'm supposed to do up there. When were you going to tell me about this?"

"Look, do you want to help Jonah or not?" Christa demanded.

"Of course, I do but what about the rest of the FBI? Have you called in backup yet? I want to help but wouldn't there be someone better qualified?"

"I haven't told anyone back at headquarters," Christa admitted, biting her lip and glancing through the window at the casino floor. "I don't want to risk Jonah getting in trouble. He wasn't supposed to go alone. We wouldn't want him to lose his job, so we have to do this together."

"Do what?"

"Tonight at the masquerade we have to catch the attention of Mr. X."

"Mr. X? Is that even a real name?" Sloane asked.

"No, but no one knows who he really is. He's the one Jonah was meeting with when he disappeared. And this hotel's namesake if you catch my drift. I never had contact with him since Jonah insisted on going alone.

"Either one of us could catch his eye but the only way I could figure on getting his attention was to parade the one and only 'expert' paranormal real-estate agent in front of him. Then we have to look the part at the ball and hopefully we'll get an invite to his room. So, what I need you to do is step up and take one for the team. Can't you sit on a panel and talk about all your ghost mumbo-jumbo for a couple of hours to save Jonah?"

"Yes…I mean, I will, but really…*that's* your plan. It's pretty shitty and seems like a long shot. What is the topic of discussion on this panel anyway?"

"I don't know. The front desk cutie gave me a folder you can look them over while I'm giving you your makeover,"

"Wait, what?"

"You can't sit on the panel or go to a ball looking like this, now can you, Cinder-Sloane? Let's get moving."

The elevator stopped and the door dinged open. Christa breezed through, stopping in front of a door and pulling out the key card.

"By the way, I could only get one room. I had our bags moved here from our other location. It's under your name and I used your credit card."

"Are you kidding me? How did you get my credit card number? Never mind, don't answer that," she lifted a hand to rub the ache forming in her temples. "Shouldn't the FBI be paying for this?"

"Not if we don't want them to know about Jonah. If anyone asks, I'm your manager and we've been dating for years."

"But weren't you supposed to be married to Jonah?"

"He went off on his own to make the deal with Mr. X. No one involved has any idea who I am. But if you want to solidify the story, I can go into great detail about all of my quirks in bed." With a wink, the blonde bombshell held open the door.

"Seriously, you have issues. And you are so not my type." Sloane muttered as she pushed past.

"I have issues?" Christa gave a warm, tinkley laugh. "I'm not the one who searches for ghosts for a living."

The room was bigger than her apartment and three times the size of the suite she'd just abandoned in St. Louis. It had one king size bed with an emerald duvet cover and at least a dozen different shaped pillows in bright jeweled tones. The drapes were thrown open, letting in the light and showing off a view of the Strip. There was a sitting area with a couple of couches and a giant television. Christa and Jonah's bags were already piled next to the bed with several shopping bags from high end stores she'd never heard of but sounded expensive.

"I'm so tired, I don't know if I can even keep my eyes open for a panel discussion with a bunch of strangers."

Not even bothering to change before climbing into the bed, Christa tossed pillows in every direction. At least she slid off the high heels before she patted the bed next to her. "I've already asked for a wakeup call at three. We can get ready for the panel then," she said, covering her mouth as she yawned. "That's a nice three-hour nap for us."

"Are we sharing?" Sloane asked, eyeing the single bed.

"Unless you want to sleep on the floor," Christa replied. "Don't worry, I don't bite. And I'm too tired to do anything but rest."

She debated for a moment before grabbing one of the pillows Christa had tossed on the floor and climbing into bed. She was too tired to fight anymore. Punching her pillow into shape, she turned her back on Christa closing her eyes and praying for sleep.

****

When the phone rang for their wakeup call, Sloane wasn't ready to get up. She never woke up well because it took her so long to fall asleep in the first place. And three short hours didn't feel like enough. She groaned, rolling away from the phone and pulling her pillow over her head to block her ears.

Christa, however, crawled across Sloane to answer, putting an elbow in Sloane's spleen and grabbing her right boob in the process. After replacing the receiver, still half draped over Sloane's body, Christa took annoying to the next level by prodding her in the side with a finger.

"Wakey, wakey," she said.

"No," Sloane grumbled.

"No?" Christa asked. "I think you meant to say, yes. Now get out of bed. I only have two hours to get you ready for the panel. The masquerade starts immediately after, so we'll have to do a quick change to get you ready for that."

"Christa, I don't have anything to wear to this panel, let alone a ball so I'm not sure how you think this is going to happen." She gave in and sat up, eyeing the blonde who looked like a freshly coiffed, dewey-faced model with disdain. Every hair was in place and there weren't even wrinkles in her clothes.

"Don't worry." She waved a hand in dismissal as she went back to her side of the bed where her stack of bags still rested. "I knew you wouldn't have anything appropriate, so I made a call and had clothes delivered for both of us. Jonah and I were staying elsewhere and seeing as I've never met Mr. X officially, he'd have no reason to recognize me or connect me with Jonah."

Digging through the shopping bags and throwing things onto the bed. Sloane saw sequins, slinky lingerie, stiletto heels, and lots of black. Finally, Christa emerged clutching a provocative pink dress, that shimmered in the light. She held it up to herself and Sloane smothered a grimace.

"You're nuts if you think I'm going to wear that,"

Sloane said, crossing her arms over her chest.

"Of course you're not, silly. I am," Christa laughed. "You couldn't pull this off if you wanted to. Here's what I have for you. I figured you're a four, but I have something else if this doesn't work."

She handed her a black strapless knee-length dress made of a silky material that slid between Sloane's fingers.

"Ok, I guess I like this," Sloane admitted.

"I told the shoppers your style. It's like glamour goth so you've got this. There's a jacket you can wear to the panel that matches. But first, you need a complete makeover."

"Thanks a lot."

"Don't thank me until we're done and the both of us get invited up to Mr. X's room so we can get a clue to help find out what happened to Jonah."

From another suitcase, which turned out to be more of a giant cosmetic bag, Christa pulled out enough make-up and hair paraphernalia for an entire Miss America pageant. She laid it out in neat rows on the bed like instruments of torture, pulling a chair and motioning for Sloane to sit.

"I thought you were an FBI agent, not a makeup artist," Sloane said.

"Do you know how many personas an undercover agent has to be able to create?" Christa asked, starting to work on brushing Sloane's hair. "This is all part of the job. Plus, I'm not stupid. I know what I look like. People don't take pretty girls like us seriously, so I play it up and use it to my advantage. Plus, it's fun to be the girly agent especially with so many good-looking men with rock hard abs around the office. I can be eye candy and still lethal all at once."

"I can see that," Sloane replied, watching as Christa began heating a straightening iron and a curling wand. What could she possibly be doing with both of those? "What are we up against here with Mr. X?"

"From what I've been able to dig up since Jonah disappeared, this guy is the worst of the worst. Power hungry, rich, and eccentric, which lets him do whatever he wants with the money he has. One of his hobbies is collecting 'haunted' items. Complete waste of his fortune if you ask me."

"Haunted items?" Sloane's ears perked up. "Are we talking like the Annabelle doll or haunted paintings?"

"I'm sure he has some of those, but mostly he likes weapons and implements of torture that have a sordid past. He seems to have his fingers in a lot of different pots, from laundering money to human trafficking." Christa ran the straightening iron through Sloane's straight hair, making it shine. "We just can't pin any of it to him so we can't bring him in. We've been watching him for years and Jonah and I had finally gotten close. After meetings with several people, we finally heard his name a few times while posing as a married couple selling our haunted collection.

"Mr. X. asked for a sit-down with only Jonah. No 'wives.' So I've never seen the guy. But then Jonah goes to meet with him and never comes back. That's where you come in. You're my ticket to the paranormal elite. By the way, here's a list of the panel questions. Look over them while you have time."

Christa handed her a folder to peruse and while Sloane read, she got quiet and focused on her with what

Sloane considered "implements of torture", not only straightening but then curling Sloane's hair (what's the point in that?) but also attacking her face with a bunch of pointy brushes.

When she finished, she took a step back to admire her work, then smiled.

"I hope you like it. I gave you a kind of a smoky look to go with the dress. Now slip it on while I get ready."

Sloane grabbed the dress and headed for the bathroom. No way was she getting naked in front of Christa after the bathtub in St. Louis and she was positive nothing was going to fit underneath the silky strapless. She slipped the silky fabric over her head, enjoying the feel of it sliding down her body. Glancing in the mirror, she was surprised by what she saw.

Christa had done a good job. She'd highlighted Sloane's cheekbones, so they stood out against her pale skin. Her eyes were hazy with dark gray and black shadow and she'd never seen her eyelashes as long as they were now. Make-up really could do wonders when applied correctly. Who knew?

Her hair was a mass of curls pulled to one side to cascade over one shoulder. Every single hair was perfectly in place as if there was no way one dark lock would disobey Christa's command.

By the time Sloane exited the bathroom, Christa was ready to go. How the blonde had managed to do her hair and makeup in a few short minutes, Sloane didn't know. The girl looked amazing in the shimmering pink dress. The slit went up her left leg to her mid-thigh, showing off a generous amount of toned leg.

She pulled on the jacket and slipped into the high heeled shoes she needed to finish her outfit, hurrying after Christa as she headed for the elevator. Sloane's nerves kicked in as elevator took them down to the second floor and the X-emplar Board Room where the panel was being held. The jacket made her feel much more business-like and she was grateful for the addition when they got down to the room.

"Ok, do your thing," Christa said, when they reached the door. "I'll meet you back at the room when you're done, right?"

"Not a problem," Sloane said. "What are you going to do?"

"Recon and a little flirting to get my way," Christa smiled, showing off her straight white teeth and Sloane had to smile back. The girl was pretty funny in her own way. Christa winked and blew her a kiss, leaving her with a final whisper in her ear, "Try not to get yourself killed, I might need you later."

Chapter 5

Christa left her at the door to the panel, practically sprinting down the hall. How she managed to run in heels, Sloane didn't know but the girl could move.

Taking a deep breath and squaring her shoulders, she headed into the room and toward the dais. There were already a few people scattered about in the chairs, but the room was mostly empty. Making her way onto the platform, she took a seat behind her name, glancing at the panel questions again.

"Sloane Osborne?" A man's hand appeared in front of her face and she shook it without thinking. "I have to admit, I was excited when I learned you were a last-minute addition to this panel. I'm a big fan of your work."

She turned to him, intending to smile and say thank you but froze. For some reason she'd forgotten how to breathe, let alone speak. The man smiled, a dimple showing in only his right cheek as released her, going to take his seat at the other table.

"That was Jack Sackins, The TV star!" She breathed, talking to herself. He was the most amazing paranormal investigator/tv hottie/author/explorer of all things paranormal ever. And he knew her name!

She wasn't really sure how she fit in with the "expert" panel but if he was a fan of her work she must belong.

Other than her, there were five people on the panel. Two tables sat on a raised platform with the proctor's podium in the middle. At one table there was an author of the latest craze in werewolf/vampire horror stories, Jack Sackins, and a clairvoyant, who claimed to be able to speak with ghosts like Whoopie Goldberg had done in that movie from the eighties.

At her table, she was wedged between the director of a horror film due out in the fall and the curator of a small paranormal museum in Las Vegas.

The director, all polished and presentable in his designer suit and diamond tie pin with matching cufflinks took his seat and promptly ignored her, keeping his focus on the tablet in front of him while also talking on his earpiece. She knew better than to try talking to him. He obviously didn't have time for anyone but himself.

A weaselly older man in a brown tweed suit smelling of mothballs and chicken soup body odor slid into the spot next to her, wiping his sopping brow with a yellowed handkerchief.

"You must be Ms. Osborne," he said, extending his other hand.

"It's Sloane," she said, giving his hand a firm shake. "You must be Mr. Finch. I've heard about your museum. I've always wanted to go, but this is my first trip to Las Vegas, and I haven't had time yet."

"Angus," he replied. "And it's no hurry. The items in my museum aren't going anywhere."

"I was surprised to see your name card here," she said. "I must have missed your name on the billing in the lobby."

"You didn't miss it. They didn't include me until

this morning. I'm local and I'm cheap so I'm always the one they call when someone doesn't show, or they need another live body."

The way he said the word "body" was kind of creepy and she felt goosebumps rise on her arms. That hadn't happened since Wisconsin. She knew she was safe enough with the number of people filing into the room, but it brought back bad memories. At least she knew better than to trust strange old men now.

"Well, I'm glad you could make it," she said with an uneasy smile.

"Why is that?" Angus asked.

"Now I won't be the strangest person on the panel," she replied, only half joking.

To her surprise the old man wheezed a laugh sounding a little too much like Alvin Mitchell for comfort. Alvin had been instrumental in her abduction in Wisconsin when she'd almost died. She reached for the pitcher of water on the table, suddenly parched. She poured herself a glass, drinking it down in one gulp before pouring another.

Her eyes glued to the growing audience she couldn't miss when a man in an odd-looking bowler hat sat down in the front row. His head was down so she couldn't see his face, but something about him...

"Ladies and gentlemen! Welcome to Para-Sin, the greatest paranormal conference in Las Vegas." A female moderator stepped onto the platform by the tables. She was rail thin and dressed like Elvira from the outrageous black wig to the extensive cleavage. Sloane took another drink of water. This was going to be a long session.

"As you know, this is the question and answer

panel, where you can ask any question you have about paranormal activity. We are joined today by a variety of different professionals who I know you are all excited to learn more about. And now, the introductions. Let's start with our resident celebrity, Mr. Jack Sackins!"

The applause was thunderous, and it was obvious who everyone was here to see. The room had filled completely, leaving many people standing in the back. Sloane felt her palms start to sweat. Why had she agreed to this? She wasn't a speaker. Why would they even have wanted her on the panel? She wanted to get up and walk away but instead waved with a slight smile when her turn to be introduced came around.

"All right then," the woman continued. "We'll start with one of our submitted questions to get the discussion moving."

Elvira pulled a pile of notecards out of her pocket and read the first question.

"Have you ever seen a ghost and if so, who was it and when? Let's start with our paranormal real-estate agent, since we know she's seen a ghost." The woman laughed as if there was something funny about that comment. "Ms. Osborne, could you tell us about your first contact."

Sloane took a deep breath, feeling heat rise to her face as she began to talk about that house in Wisconsin and how she'd known she'd find him there.

Michael. It always came back to Michael. Her first love. Her fiancé. And the death of the man she was going to marry.

She and Michael had gotten into a car accident on the way to get their marriage license. A part of her had died that day and it had taken a complete change in her life, combining her new real-estate license with her love of ghost hunting, to help her get over the loss.

And Jonah. Michael's best friend who'd admitted he'd loved her all along. Now there was a chance she'd lose him too. She couldn't let that happen.

She poured herself another glass of water, surprised to find her glass empty again. Every time she thought about Wisconsin she got thirsty. Being trapped in a tomb of ghosts who died from dehydration wasn't something a girl forgot about very easily.

The panel passed in a barrage of questions she didn't always know the answer to or even agree with. Jack, being his charismatic self, kept the audience on the edge of their seats with every answer. The author ended all of his answers with a not so subtle plug for his book. The director seemed more interested in his phone than the interview but managed to muster his attention to answer a question or two about how to get into the horror movie business. And the clairvoyant guy was vague to the point of being a jerk. She thought he sounded like an idiot, but the audience ate it up.

The one who surprised her was Angus. It was obvious he'd done these kinds of panels before. He was animated and funny, even if he did seem paranoid about the government monitoring him and brought up a few conspiracy theories. The people seemed to love him. She could picture him leading tours through his museum telling patrons about each item with a detailed, spine chilling story.

"All right," Elvira said, standing next to the table and pulling down on her skirt, which covered her bottom but only managed to show more cleavage. "We have time for one more question. I'll direct this to our

Las Vegas native, Mr. Finch. Sir, what is the most dangerous haunted item you have ever dealt with?"

The old man's face, that had been open and jovial turned suddenly dark. A frown turned down the edges of his lips and his bushy white eyebrows crinkled together as if threatening to become one.

"The Twin Blades of Butchery, of course," he said.

The room went silent as every ear turned to Angus, waiting for him to speak. When he didn't Elvira glanced nervously at him.

"I'm sorry, I must have forgotten to ask for an explanation, silly me," she laughed as if the uncomfortable silence was her fault. "Could you tell us about these blades?"

"Yes, do." The director's attention was off his tablet and on Angus' face. "I'm very interested in how they came to be in your possession."

"If you've heard of them, you'll know they aren't an easy topic to discuss. I bought them from a man who claimed they were cursed before I knew exactly what they were. I owned the blades for a short time. Very short, but at the same time much too long. They cost me more than I ever wanted to pay."

Sloane's interest was piqued as well. She'd never heard of the Twin Blades of Butchery.

"I know about these knives," the author said, steepling his fingers in front of his face as he leaned forward onto the table. "I researched them for one of my books. I believe they were made in Italy in the 15th century. Is that right?"

Angus nodded, his eyes hooded, and he suddenly looked like a different person. He looked conflicted, almost as if he wanted nothing more than to have the blades back again, even though he appeared to say differently.

"One of the blades has ruby stones set into the hilt and the other sapphires," the author continued. "They have a tragic story. I believe they were stolen from the original owners and disappeared for years. Each time they've surfaced since, they are associated with at least one but sometimes two brutal murders, and usually between lovers."

"Ooo, lovers?" Elvira gasped. "Always?"

"Usually a married couple, but also a man and his mistress. After each murder they are usually reported stolen or go missing again and when they're found it's almost always in the bodies of a man and his wife."

The whole room was silent, hanging on the author's every word.

"Is this all true?" The director cleared his throat, ignoring the pinging on his tablet. "And you owned these blades, Finch?"

Angus nodded. "They are deceptively beautiful and when you hold them, it's as if you can feel their power in your veins. Only they don't care what you want to do with the power. All they want is to find the one you love and slice into their heart. Each and every day I wonder how I am still alive and regret…."

He trailed off making Sloane wonder who he'd loved when he'd owned the knives.

"Do you know where they are now?" she asked. "Who did you sell them to?"

"I have no idea. I didn't sell them. I tried to hide them, thinking it would be safer for the world if I did, but one day they were just…gone." He waved his hand, making a poofing motion like something disappearing into thin air. "I wish I did know who had them so I could warn them. Those knives are dangerous and should be dealt with properly. I was researching how to dispose of them and if they hadn't disappeared, I would have taken care of it. I should have before it was too late."

She watched as the man in the front row with the bowler hat suddenly stood. He tipped his hat to her in an old-fashioned gesture before turning toward the exit.

"So, you're sure you don't have any idea who has them?" The author had a greedy look in his eye she didn't like.

"He just said he didn't," she said, defending Finch. "And if any of you were paying attention, you'd realize he doesn't want to talk about them anymore. With the history of the knives, I can understand why."

And suddenly she did understand. If he'd owned the knives, it was quite possible someone he loved had died. She and Angus had a connection.

"All right, well, I think that's about all we have time for today," Elvira said in a shaky voice, drawing the crowd's attention away from the panel and back to her. "I'm sure everyone needs time to freshen up before the masquerade tonight. Let's have a round of applause for our amazing panel and the excellent discussion we had tonight!"

When the applause tapered off and people began filing from the room, Sloane turned to Angus as he pulled himself to his feet. He looked as tired as she felt. She was not a people person and being put on show had been exhausting.

She felt as if her soul had been dragged through the Las Vegas gutter, sent for a tumble down the Colorado

River, and slammed against the Hoover Dam a few times before being pulled back like a fish on a line. She wanted pizza, ice cream, a bath, and a good cry. Maybe not in that order. Instead she turned to Angus with a smile.

"It was great meeting you," she said.

"You too, my dear." He reached into his wallet and pulled out a card. "If you have a spare moment, please feel free to stop by my museum." He reached into his wallet and pulled out a card, then started a sing-songy jingle in an off-key tone. "If you want a good scare while you're in town, try Finch's House on Fourth and Crown."

"Thanks, I might do that," Sloane lied, tucking the card into her purse. "Right now, I guess I have a ball to attend, whether I want to or not."

"Oh, to be young and spry again," the man laughed. "Do try to have fun for us old codgers who don't get out very often."

"I'll do my best," she said with a wave as she made her exit.

She made a quick jaunt to the room where there was no sign of Christa, just a note next to a small black demi-mask made of small swirls of metal shaped to look like lace.

Something came up. I'll meet you at the ball. Don't forget your mask.

Sloane slipped off her jacket before securing the mask over her eyes. She sighed, looking at herself in the mirror. She didn't look like herself at all.

As she stepped out into the hallway, she swore she saw the man in the bowler hat turn a corner down the hallway. Was it the one from the audience at the panel?

She started after him but stopped herself. She needed to think about Jonah and right now Christa needed her help.

Squaring her shoulders, she pressed the button for the elevator that would take her to her first ball.

The ballroom was decorated in swaths of black and white silk, hanging from the ceiling in long elegant drapes and covering the tables. The room was entirely lit by candles. There wasn't a single electric light in the room. It looked amazing but was certainly a fire hazard.

Couples danced in the center of the room, but not in the old-fashioned way she imagined would happen at a ball. They didn't waltz but instead swayed in time to the music, like a costumed wedding party.

All around her were masks. Some were more elaborate than the tiny thing covering half her face but there were plenty of demi-masks like her own. She spotted several phantoms of the opera, some swashbuckling Musketeers and there were princesses and faeries in abundance.

Her stomach rumbling, she made a beeline for the food table and grabbed a small plate of cucumber sandwiches and a couple chocolate bon-bons before being interrupted.

"Sloane Osborne, right?" the man said, sliding around between her and the food table.

She wanted to growl but tried to be polite. He looked young, maybe in college, and was wearing a court jester outfit she wasn't sure if he thought was fashionable or just fit his personality.

"I thought the point of a masquerade was so you wouldn't know who anyone was," she said, reaching around the lad for another sandwich.

"True, but I recognized your hair. You had it styled already at the panel."

Damn Christa and her handiwork. Now everyone was going to know who she was. And all because of a hairdo.

"What can I do for you?" she asked.

"Well, I wanted to talk to you about ghosts," the young man said, his smile never leaving his face. "Are you aware that by claiming you see ghosts you are inviting the devil into your life and leading a life of sin?"

Oh, he was one of those. *Perfect.* Why did people go to conventions like this if they didn't believe in any of it? Didn't they have better things to spend their money on?

"A life of sin? Funny to hear me accused of that, especially in this city."

"But don't you think you're going to hell?"

"I thought being judgmental of others was also a sin," she said. "Something about 'he without sin should cast the first stone' or something. Are you telling me you are completely without any sin in your life?"

He opened his mouth, floundering for a moment, and she seized on his indecision.

"That's what I thought," she said. "Now if you'll excuse me, I think I see my friend."

It wasn't a lie. Christa was hard to miss in her pink shimmering dress with a look-at-me slit up one side. Crowds stared and heads turned as she sauntered across the room and Sloane could see why. Even with half her face covered with a lacy pink and black mask, she was the epitome of a man's desired sin. Ironic that Sloane was being accused of sinning when she looked nothing like that.

A pang hit her in the chest. Did Jonah have thoughts of lust when he was around her? The thought alone was enough to have her lift her chin and approach the woman determined to prove herself worthy.

She started toward her when she felt a chill down her spine. It was as if someone had just walked over her grave. Her breath caught and she froze in place. Goosebumps sprang up on her arms and felt the cold seep into her bones. She turned slowly to find a gentleman staring at her.

He was dressed in all black from his wing tip shoes to the mask covering his face. His clothes were tailored specifically for him, black designer pants, a black shirt, and tie covered by a black jacket. He didn't have any adornments except the gold-topped black cane he carried in one hand. His hair was slicked back and gelled so not one strand of the salt and pepper locks was out of place. Flanking him were two muscled men who almost looked like dark shadows.

Both men wore gray suits with bulges around their waists, letting her know they were the embodiment of the line 'armed and dangerous.' One of the men was white with slicked black hair, built like a lineman with a neck thicker than her thigh. The other was black and at least six foot eight with his head shaved so close it looked like he was made of polished ebony.

All three of them stared at her.

"There you are," Christa said, rushing over and grabbing her arm. She spun her until she was no longer facing the man in black, but she could still feel his eyes on her. "I've been looking everywhere for you. I need a drink. Do you need a drink?"

Christa linked her arm through hers and led her to the nearby bar.

"Nice work, my girl," she whispered, leaning close. "That's Mr. X behind you flanked by bodyguards. It seems you've already caught his attention."

"But why? I mean, I'm pretty amazing but why would he single out me?"

"He collects paranormal oddities. My guess is he considers you one too."

That didn't reassure her at all.

"But…" she began.

"His reasons don't matter right now. What matters is we're in. My recon worked. He is the man we're looking for and I saw him peeking in at the panel and I thought he was staring at you. This is good."

"This isn't good," she said, finding her voice. "He's evil. I can feel it coming off of him."

"You're probably right," Christa replied, her smile turning stern. "But this guy's our only lead to find Jonah. You need to remember that."

One of the muscled guards approached them, sliding an envelope onto the bar in front of Sloane before walking away. She opened it with trembling fingers, finding a simple invitation printed in gold ink of black paper.

Mr. X—Executive Suite—Floor 40.

When she turned around, they were gone.

"Seriously? Who prints an invite to their hotel room?" she asked. "That's creepy. Does he stay here a lot?"

"He owns the hotel, honey," Christa replied.

"He owns the hotel? You didn't tell me that! Why didn't you tell me? Though it does explain the unusual amount of x words used to name everything." Out of the corner of her eye, she was sure she saw the man in a bowler hat again. He was staring right at her. She raised her brows in question, and he smiled, tipping his hat before disappearing into the crowd.

"I must have told you, but it doesn't matter. Even if it seems too easy and, on a normal day, neither one of us would want to go anywhere near him. This is our ticket to Jonah. Are you ready?"

For Jonah?

She nodded, though it felt like this was probably the worst decision she'd ever made. For Jonah she'd do anything.

Chapter 6

Sloane knocked gently on the door to Mr. X's suite. It looked like any other door in the hotel, expect this one was the only door on the floor. Once she got off the elevator, there wasn't any possibility she could get lost.

She toyed with the fabric on her dress, so nervous she felt like throwing up or laughing hysterically, neither of which were going to be any help with locating and rescuing Jonah. She really wished she wasn't on her own.

Even though she wasn't in Vegas alone, like she usually was at one of her real-estate jobs, she was solo now. Christa had made her go by herself, insisting she had a plan and would come up when, "the time was right". *Whatever that meant.*

The door to the lion's den squeaked quietly when it was opened by the white bodyguard with the slicked black hair and muscles bulging beneath his designer gray suit. He gestured her inside with the sort of half-smile that didn't seem very genuine.

She wondered what he would do if she mussed his locks like she would a toddler. Would he laugh, smack her with one of his ham-hands, or pull the gun she saw holstered at his waist when his jacket shifted? Resisting the urge, she followed him into the room.

Inside, it was like no other hotel room she'd ever

seen. It had an entry with a white marble table adorned with dozens of fresh white roses and pink and white lilies, their stamens dripping with orangey-yellow pollen. Together their perfumes tickled her nostrils, the floral scent almost too much to bear. It made her nauseous and gave her a headache immediately, like when she got too close to an older woman wearing enough perfume to drown in the scent.

"This way," the bulky man said, leading her to long living space with floor to ceiling windows and a door leading out to a balcony overlooking the entire Vegas Strip. She could see the lights flashing on the replica Eiffel tower and could even make out the spectacle of the epic water and light show going on at the Bellagio fountains.

Mr. X rose off a white leather sofa turned to face a wall of flat screen monitors as she entered, his movements smooth and precise, like a stalking tiger. He snapped his fingers at one of his underlings. She jumped when she heard a loud POP.

"Pour a glass of champagne for Miss Osborne." Mr. X oozed and immediately the black guard with the shiny head brought him a flute of bubbling liquid. He held it out to her. The sound of his slimy voice put her on edge. Here stood a man used to getting what he wanted, and at the moment, he wanted her in his private room. She had no idea why.

Well, that wasn't true. She had some guesses.

And those guesses were reminding her she really needed to sign up for some sort of self-defense class when this was all over. And maybe learn to shoot a gun. Who would have thought that would come in handy as a paranormal real-estate agent? She wanted to *work* with dead people not become one herself.

Even though she knew she was completely in over her head, she took a deep breath, and stared him straight in the eye. She may be small and untrained, but if this guy had hurt Jonah in any way, she'd poke out his beady, little eyeballs herself.

"No, thank you. You're sweet to offer but I've learned the hard way not to take drinks from strangers. Perhaps once I get to know you, I'll feel better about the drink." She took it from him, setting the stemmed glass on the table in front of her before easing onto the black leather couch.

"I can accept that," Mr. X said, pouring himself a drink of dark amber liquid over ice. "I'll do what I can to make you feel more comfortable."

If he only knew how uncomfortable those words made her.

"In that case, answer me this: why am I here, Mr...?" she paused, cocking her head to the side as she examined him. "I simply refuse to call you Mr. X. Tell me your name."

"Can't a man simply desire a woman's company?"

"A man could, but I doubt that's why I'm here," she replied, rolling her eyes and looking away.

To her surprise, he laughed and made a shooing motion with one hand. The two guards backed away, leaving them alone.

"I'm delighted to discover you *are* the shrew everyone says. I love that. Call me Xavier, then if it pleases you." He approached her slowly, gliding along the floor. He exuded an air of indifference, but she knew there was a reason she was invited here. He wanted something from her. And that was fine. As long as she also got something in return…Jonah.

In spite of her refusal before, she reached forward and grabbed the bubbling flute of champagne and took a tentative sip, more to dispel her shrewness than anything else. She doubted it was drugged. A man like him wouldn't think he needed to resort to such measures. Or at least that's what she told herself.

"All right, *Xavier*." He had pronounced it the French way, so it sounded like it started with a z and not a x. "Point for you, but I'm not a shrew. I'm cautious. You would be too if you'd been through what I have. And by the way, who's *everyone?* I need to go kick some asses."

He laughed and slid open the door to the patio. She followed him outside. The air was still hot, but the wind made it warm instead of stifling. It felt good after the cool air-conditioned temperature inside, as if it was thawing her, giving her strength and keeping her senses sharp.

Though she did notice her hair wasn't moving in the nighttime breeze. Christa and all that damn hairspray

Not that Xavier's hair moved either. He had enough gel in there to cement his follicles together.

"Why am I here, Xavier?" she asked, leaning against the railing and staring at the Strip. "There are hundreds of people down there and yet you singled me out and invited only me to your room. Why is that?"

"You're a beautiful woman. Why wouldn't you believe I simply wanted a chance to get to know you?" he asked, sliding over to stand beside her.

She felt the hairs raise on her arms, the same as they would for a ghost. This man was creepy. Every word he said seemed shrouded in mystery. She couldn't tell when he was being truthful or lying through his teeth and nothing about the situation made her feel safe. She felt almost as vulnerable as she had stuck in the hole in Wisconsin with a serial killer staring down at her.

"You just called me a shrew. I'd say it's a safe bet we both know my company isn't worth your time."

"All right, then, why do you think you're here?" he asked, leaning against the ledge, his posture nonchalant though his eyes burned with a challenge. She could see he wanted to know her answer.

"I heard a rumor you collect paranormal objects. I happen to be a paranormal real-estate agent, and a good one. Perhaps you're looking to buy a haunted house?"

"No, but heading in the right direction," he laughed. "I've acquired a unique set of haunted items I want your personal opinion on. I'm having some trouble with them as they may have more value and power..." he lingered over the word *power* and she couldn't even begin to wonder what the word meant to him, "...than I've ever encountered. I am loath to say, these pieces scare even me. I would like your help discovering what they are truly capable of."

Now he had her attention. What in the world could he have?

"There are a lot of more qualified people at this conference who could help you," she replied. "I sell haunted houses. I'm not trained to give you the value of an item or to deal with curses. I think you'd need some sort of shaman for that."

He lit a cigarette and inhaled deeply before letting out a thin stream of smoke the air gobbled up in scant seconds. She wrinkled her nose in disgust at the scent streaming into the night air. Turning away, she stared at the lights down the Strip, wishing she was at any of the other hotels. The one with the Eiffel Tower looked nice. They probably had good desserts at that one.

"I can't involve shamans. Or priests. I have certain…clients, let's call them," Xavier explained. "They pay me handsomely for certain types of entertainments. Things they wouldn't want others to know about if you catch my meaning. Discretion is crucial for my business."

"How do you know I'll be discreet?"

"Because I know quite a bit about you, Miss Osborne. For instance, a little bird told me you've been operating without a valid real-estate license for some time now."

She whipped her head around to face him. Seriously? Was another person going to blackmail her?

"Holy hell, how does everyone but me know my license expired?"

His smile was smooth. "As I said, a little bird told me, but I'm certain anything we discuss here will remain just between the two of us."

She wondered if he was talking about the child trafficking Christa had mentioned or if this was something else. She forced back her revulsion trying to appear interested, though perplexed by his words. "You are being a bit too vague though, but that's probably intentional. And I'm not sure what games can be played with haunted objects."

"Come," he flicked his half-smoked cigarette over the balcony, and she could only imagine what someone on the ground would think when it smacked them in the head. He grabbed her wrist, pulling her back inside. "Since you keep asking, let me show you exactly why you're here."

He led her back through the doors and into a living room. The two guards had returned, standing completely still against opposite walls, their arms crossed over their chests and identical expressions of attentive boredom on their faces.

"Please sit," Xavier said, gesturing to the stark white leather couch facing the flat screen monitors mounted on the wall. She shook her head, intending to stand.

"Suit yourself," he said, grabbing a small black remote and pushing the power button until one of the ginormous flat screens turned on.

It was fuzzy for a moment, then a live black and white feed with the corner reading the time and the date came into focus. There was no volume, but she could imagine the yelling coming from the man tied to a wooden chair with a black canvas bag over his head as he struggled against his bonds.

An object she couldn't identify—maybe a knife or an elaborate piece of jewelry—sat on a table in front of him glittering in the pale light. As she watched, the man began to convulse and throw back his head as if he were in pain.

Could it be Jonah? Her heart raced.

Before she could ask, there was a knock on the door.

"Get rid of them, whoever it is," Xavier ordered.

The brutish looking guard nodded once before disappearing toward the door.

"Room servicing," a singsong voice rang out when

the door opened. She heaved a sigh of relief. "Ozzy, I heard you were up here, sweetie."

"You'll have to leave, Miss," the burly guard snorted.

"Leave. I can't leave. You have my Ozzy and she and I do everything together if you catch my meaning."

Christa was being Christa, and she used their confusion to shimmy past the guard and around the marble table. When she reached Sloane, Christa grabbed her chin with one hand and planted a kiss on her lips.

"Miss me, baby? Don't you even consider having a man in the mix without me, you naughty girl." She gave Sloane a playful slap on the cheek then revealed more leg longitude than necessary when she turned to face Xavier. "Well, well, well. You can't invite a lady to your room and ignore her girlfriend, silly." She tapped him on the nose. "What does a girl have to do to get a drink around here? I'm parched."

Xavier, though clearly put out by Christa's intrusion, poured another flute of champagne and handed it to her with a smug smile.

The bodyguards' jaws hung low as they stared at Christa. Neither could seem to miss the amount of skin she was showing giving Sloane a wide-open window into the base thoughts in their dirty minds.

"Chrissy, I'm busy," she hissed, as if she wasn't happy to see the girl, jerking her shoulder away from the distracted guard.

Xavier hit a button on a remote and the screen with maybe-Jonah clicked off. His face softened. "Lovely. A threesome. Or a lover's quarrel? Either way, it works to my benefit. Come to think of it, I have some time to kill, among other things. I am not opposed to some entertainment before needing Miss Osborne's assistance on another matter," he winked at her.

"Another matter? He's not talking about stupid Jonah and your ghost hunting again. You don't have to go looking for trouble. You promised me you were done with him," Christa whined, pulling her lip out in a delicate pout. "It's you and me now. Or maybe you, new guy, and me. As long as the booze is flowing, I'm always interested in switching things up a bit. But before that, we need a moment in the powder room. Come on baby, I smeared your lipstick. I'll re-apply it."

Xavier pointed. "Second door on the left but hurry. We have much to…discuss."

Chapter 7

Sloane rushed to follow Christa to the bathroom, shutting the door and locking it once they were inside. She rounded on Christa intending to flounce the girl, but Christa held up a finger to Sloane's lips and rang her fingers under the bathroom counter, around the mirror and behind the toilet. She pulled out a small black dot and pointed outside the bathroom and then to her ear implying, *"He's listening to us."*

Sloane understood she had to play along. "Baby, I have to help him. He's an old lover and you have nothing to do with it. You should go. I told you my job can be dangerous."

With a quick roll of her eyes, Christa made a James Bond pose and pretended to shoot a gun. "Danger is my middle name. I don't mind. Besides, we never have fun as a couple anymore and this rich guy could be the key to a most excellent night." Christa wrenched up her skirt and showed Sloane the knife concealed on her upper thigh and winked. "Remember what they say about Vegas. But before I apply that lipstick, I need a little of you myself."

Christa reached for her, laughing when Sloane backed away. She'd do a lot of things for Jonah, but she wasn't engaging in any kind of hanky-panky with those gross men in the other room. Or Christa for that matter.

What if she didn't have a choice?

But this *was* Jonah they were talking about. Wouldn't she do anything to save him?

She froze with the soft tapping on the bathroom door. Someone was going to come in. She didn't know what to do. Should she stay where she was and let whoever it is figure out she hadn't been making out with Christa or should she control her gag reflex and kiss Christa?

"Hurry up in there," a deep voice called through the door before she had a chance to make up her mind. "Mr. X doesn't like to be kept waiting."

"We're just finishing up," Christa called, turning on the water to drown out their voices.

"What are we supposed to do now?" Sloane demanded in a harsh whisper. "I don't know why you followed me here. Now X thinks we're going to 'service' him. We can't waste time with him here. He has Jonah and he's torturing him. I saw it on the screen. Besides, no offense but I'm not into you, and I don't think I can handle anything like that."

Christa studied her, her eyes narrowing as she scanned her from head to toe and back again. She nodded her head slightly, and Sloane let out a deep breath, knowing Christa had figured out what she already knew. There was no way she would be able to do this.

"Geez, I can't believe you're not into me. I'm gorgeous," Christa teased. "But in all seriousness, I know what you're saying. We come from different worlds."

A world Christa shared with Jonah.

Christa didn't say the words, but she heard them loud and clear.

She hated that world.

"I'll focus on Mr. X's...*desires*, if need be," Christa breathed. "You try to get him talking about his work and the objects he collects. Maybe something he says will lead us to where he has Jonah. Can you at least handle that?"

Sloane ignored the last comment, shutting off the water and opening the door. She had better things to do than listen to Christa. Just when they'd started to get along, Christa had to turn her snotty know-it-all FBI bitch mode back on. And at the worst possible moment. Jonah's life was on the line.

They followed the dark-skinned thug with a shining bald head and sleek designer suit back to the main room. Xavier had changed while they were gone and was now reclining on the couch with one foot resting on the other knee wearing only a black silk robe monogrammed with a gold letter X.

She really hoped he didn't uncross his legs. No matter how good looking the guy was she didn't want to know what he did or did not have on under that robe. Call her a prude or 'someone from a different world' but she had no desire to find out the size of Mr. X's instrument.

The thought actually made her want to vomit.

"Come in, ladies," he motioned to them with one hand, his eyes fixed on the monitor along the wall in front of him. Back on the screen was the image of the man tied to a wooden chair in the center of a room. "Make yourselves comfortable."

Sloane glanced at the monitors and saw something was different. The center screen, the biggest tv, had the same image of the man he'd shown her before. The one she'd thought was Jonah. The other four screens all had different men, much the same circumstances. Each had a woven burlap bag over their heads and their hands were tied behind their backs. One was lying on his side, twitching uncontrollably. Sloane could see a small wooden box etched with black letters open next to him. Another was tied to a bed with a china doll resting on his chest, as if it was staring at him.

It was terrifying.

Christa shook her head at Sloane, drawing attention to her long blond locks as she sauntered into the room, sliding onto the couch beside Xavier. She crossed her legs, showing off more skin than Sloane did in her bathing suit.

Sloane opted for the chair next to the couch, hoping she'd be safe.

"Miss Osborne," Xavier drawled, reaching a hand across the back of the couch and twisting a strand of Christa's hair around one finger. "I'm very careful about who I work with. I've done my research and feel I'm sort of an expert on your history."

"My history?" Sloane echoed, confused and a little sick to her stomach.

"I know about your deceased parents and the unfortunate accident with your fiancé. I know about your job and your reputation, but I've never once heard even the whisper of a rumor about a girlfriend."

"We weren't trying to be discreet," Christa laughed, glancing at Sloane with smoldering eyes as if they shared an intimate inside joke. "We don't care. But after Sloane's rocket to fame since she got caught by those serial killers in Wisconsin and her rather unusual line of work, she wasn't itchy to splash her bi-sexual tendencies all over her stuffy real estate world. Although it might be time for a hot exposé one of these days, babe. Might jack up your business. No reason to keep our relationship or your tryst with your old ghost hunting partner a secret. When was the last time you heard from him anyway?"

Christa turned her attention to Sloane as if seriously asking her how Jonah was.

Sloane looked at Xavier, who seemed vaguely interested in how she'd answer.

"Not in a while," she replied. "I haven't heard from him in a while."

"Well, no news is good news, I always say," Christa shifted on the couch to give Xavier a better view down the front of her dress. "Especially since I get you all to myself now. However, when I hear my honey has gone to a man's hotel room all alone, that's when my protective instincts kick in. She's such a sweetheart that people always walk all over her and I wouldn't want her to get caught in a situation where she's in over her head."

Christa winked and Sloane managed a smile, though it felt more like a grimace as she tried not to jump across the armrest and wring the federal agent's pretty little neck. Why did everything Christa say sound so nice and reasonable yet come off as an insult?

Instead, she turned her attention to the center monitor, studying the would-be Jonah and ignoring Christa as she prattled on about how they'd met at a yoga class—as if Sloane had ever done yoga in her life—and about their favorite Tai restaurant in Seattle—Sloane had never been to Seattle.

She scanned the monitor to try to find a clue to

where they might be holding him. The floor beneath his feet was a mixture of rocks and sand, making Sloane wonder if it wasn't really a room, but more like a cave or a trench—something made by nature, not humans. But there were lights in the room so there had to be some sort of power source.

He was dirty, wearing a torn dress shirt and mud stained pants. And barefoot, his feet tied to the chair legs and his arms secured behind his back in what must have been an uncomfortable position. She studied him intently but there was no way to tell if it was Jonah. She couldn't judge his height from how he was sitting, and she couldn't see any discerning scars or even the shape of his hands which would have given her more of a clue.

The room was dark, except for a spotlight directed at him and the object resting on a table in front of him. The object was just out of the camera angle so she couldn't even be sure what was in the room haunting him. It looked like jewelry the way the light glinted off its surface but wasn't the right size. For some reason she kept coming back to thinking it was a knife.

And somewhere deep inside, she knew it was him. She could feel it through the strange connection the two of them had. She closed her eyes, reaching for him with her mind.

Sloane.

The word was faint in her head, but it was his voice. He was thinking of her, too.

The man on the screen sat up straighter, the tremors tearing through his body stilling.

Pain. So much pain. Stay away. Run, Sloane.

She tried to let him know she wasn't going

anywhere without him, but she wasn't sure if he heard. The man on the screen tipped his head back, the muscles in his neck pulling taught and Sloane was sure he was crying out.

There wasn't anything touching him so how could he be in pain? It didn't make any sense. Could the object in the room really be hurting him just by being there?

She had to find out.

"What's on the table?" Sloane asked, pulling Xavier's attention away from Christa.

He looked at her, his eyes unfocused for a moment as if he'd forgotten she was even in the room. She raised an eyebrow, tilting her head toward the screen and repeating her question. The man shook himself out of his stupor and smiled in appreciation.

"Haunted objects. Rather ingenious of me, don't you think? So much death is perpetrated by humans. I prefer to let the inanimate and the deceased do the work for me. These are my test subjects. It's strange how some react to these objects and others do not. I haven't quite figured out the right combination to get the effect I'm searching for but I'm confident with your help, I'll be able to achieve my goals."

"Test subject? You mean this is happening now?" Christa asked.

"Yes, these are live feeds. I study them to see the reactions to the haunted objects. I'm worried the prize of my collection might not be haunted. That's where you come in, Ms. Osborne."

"How big is your collection?"

"Want to see?" Xavier rose to his feet and put out a hand for Sloane, ignoring Christa for once.

With her heart in her throat, threatening to choke the life from her, she reached out and put her hand in his. The man's hands were as smooth as silk and she knew her palm was sweaty, her hands rough, and her nails bitten to the quicks. Why was it she could face down a house full of ghosts without batting an eye, but human beings were terrifying?

Perhaps because her track record with humans wasn't great. They either died, tried to kill her or turned out to already be dead.

He pulled Sloane to her feet, placing her hand in the crook of his elbow and led her from the room. She glanced back to see Christa rise, a dark scowl on her face. The girl was mad but at least she was following. Sloane had no desire to be alone with this man or the two large bodyguards who followed at a discreet distance.

He took them deeper into the suite and Sloane realized it was even bigger than she first suspected and was more than likely the entire 40th floor. He led them past room after room, finally pausing before the only door with an electric keypad next to the handle.

"This is where I keep a few pieces of my collection," Xavier said, dropping her arm to press his thumb to the reader before typing in a few random numbers too fast for her to catch.

"You keep it here?" she asked. "Do you live here?"

Xavier chuckled as if he found her question endearing. As if she were a puppy who needed to be taught. She wanted to smack him, but held back, clenching her hands at her sides.

"Remind me the next time someone calls you a "shrew" to correct them. You, my dear, are a charming breath of fresh air in this stale world I live in."

"Charming?" she wrinkled her nose. She didn't want this man to find her charming. "I prefer spunky."

"Spunky, yet charming. And though I spend a lot of my time here, I wouldn't call this suite my home," Xavier admitted. "But I do keep certain items here because of the security in the hotel. I have other houses around the world I visit from time to time."

"Well, let me know if you need a realtor," she replied. "I'm sure I could live for years off the commission."

"Ah, but I have a better idea for your employment, my dear." He pushed open the door, allowing them to enter the room. The two bodyguards took up positions on either side of the door.

Christa reached forward, grabbing her hand as the two of them walked in together. Sloane didn't like holding hands with the girl, but she understood the gesture. They were in this together and needed it to stay that way.

Xavier closed the door behind them, but Sloane barely even registered the action. Her eyes were focused on the strange collection before her.

The room looked like it had been pulled straight out of a museum or a jewelry store and placed in Xavier's apartment. The walls were a bright white without a hint of a cobweb or dust and the floor was tiled in black and white veined marble. Along the walls massive paintings stared at them, the painted eyes seeming to follow them as they moved like one of those old cartoon shows.

Throughout the room were glass cases full of interesting items, each with a golden plaque in front with a description. She felt goosebumps rise on her arms and the hair on the back of her neck stand on end. The room was full of paranormal activity and she wished she had some of her equipment with her to do some tests.

"Wow," Christa said, reaching for a small jewelry box. "This is a lot of stuff."

"Don't touch anything" He slapped at her hand. "I've heard there's a larger collection in the south of France, but I haven't been able to locate it," Xavier said.

Sloane made her way across the room, checking out the items under the glass. In one case there was a string of pearls on a ruby pillow, its plaque claiming they were cursed. Next to it was a shrunken head and a milky glass eye. A large black vase sat next to a pin-stuck voodoo doll, with a large sign reading 'Do Not Touch."

Across the room she saw an antique candelabra, the silver pockmarked with age, and she was pretty sure there was an actual dybbuk box or at least a replica of one. She knew the original box—a wooden cabinet with carved grapes on each door which would have been used to store wine before the malicious spirit reputed to be able to possess the living moved in—was currently owned by Jack Sackins.

"Where do you find all this stuff?" Christa asked, leaning over a cabinet holding various jewels like a purple pendant and an emerald ring. There was also a ruby encrusted knife and a golden Egyptian statue of a female goddess with wings.

"Oh, here and there," Xavier said vaguely. "Mostly private auctions but you'd be surprised how much you can find on eBay."

Sloane couldn't picture this man trolling around on eBay any more than she could fathom how someone like him had managed to capture Jonah, but since Jonah was missing, she had to keep an open mind about everything.

"It is quite the collection," she admitted, "but I really don't see what it has to do with me. Which item did you wanted my opinion on?" Sloane asked.

"Ah, you were looking at it." He gestured to the ruby encrusted knife. "I'm sure you can make it work. I'm excited to see if the stories are true."

Sloane turned back to the red and gold knife, admiring the exquisite workmanship on the jewel encrusted handle. The sliver blade curved slightly, before coming to a sharp point. She felt a pull to it, like it was begging her to grab hold of the hilt and feel the weight of it in her hand. "It's beautiful," she said. "I have no idea what it is though. I don't know why you think I'd know what to do with it. There's no way I can help you."

"Well, no. Not here, of course. I'm afraid you and the FBI agent are going to have to come with me."

Sloane ripped her gaze away from the knife to look at Xavier. Had he really said what she thought she'd heard?

"You can't be surprised I don't believe your lies, ladies. Not after my men followed Miss Christa who showed up here in Vegas with your beloved Jonah to sell me that knife. Your little act can end right now."

Panic struck a second too late. A burlap sack came over her head from behind, cutting off not only the light but the air to breathe. Immediately her throat closed off as her mouth became dry as sand. She heard a gasp next to her and knew Christa was getting the same treatment. She tried to struggle but her arms were wrenched behind her and tied with a coarse rope.

"I am sorry about this," Xavier's voice was muffled but she knew it was him. "But I'm too excited to wait another moment."

She felt him slip something into her palm and knew at once, it was the knife. A stabbing pain shot through her back and she felt like she'd been stabbed, not just handed a knife. She bent over, gasping for air when all she could pull in was the stale air in the bag. She was going to die if she panicked.

Though she was probably going to die anyway, which didn't help her panic. They were going to kill her and bury her in the desert where her body would never be found. She knew it.

She had to calm down but couldn't seem to force her heart to stop racing or her breath to rasp in and out of her throat.

"Don't say I didn't ever do you a favor." Xavier's voice was the last thing she heard before someone held a cloth over her mouth. She fought. Hard. Until everything went black.

Chapter 8

Sloane woke up with a start, her head throbbing as if someone was pounding on her forehead with a power hammer. Before she even opened her eyes, she knew she was no longer in the hotel. She could hear the hum of an engine and feel the vibrations of the vehicle below her. She opened her eyes, but still couldn't see and realized a burlap sack still covered her head.

Her throat went dry and her tongue felt like it was swelling to twice its normal size. A deep ache built in her chest and Sloane felt the panic attack begin. Her heart raced and a cold sweat broke out all over her body. Knowing she couldn't let the panic overtake her, she tried to take a deep breath, forcing herself to calm. It didn't help. She sucked the burlap sack in with the air, the surface scraping her already dry tongue.

She needed water. But there wasn't any. And Jonah wasn't going to come to save her now. It was her turn to do the saving, though it didn't look like she was doing a very good job.

She needed to focus. To think about things besides the desert growing in her throat and the sharp stabbing in her head. Put together what she knew to build a list of things she could control.

Forcing a sense of calm, she took the first step; discovering where she was.

Since she was lying flat on her back on what felt

like wooden slats, her best guess was she was in the back of a box truck. And one that had moved other living creatures recently. She could smell urine and the faint tang of unwashed bodies. The scent made her want to vomit. She rolled to her side, willing herself not to throw up inside the hood as she twisted and pulled, trying to slide her hands out of the ropes cutting into her wrists and ankles.

"Sloane, stop it." She heard Christa's voice from beside her. "Take a deep breath. Calm down, don't freak out, you'll make it worse."

"What happened?"

"They knocked us out. From the way my head feels, my best guess is they used chloroform, then tossed us in this truck. I don't know how long we've been out. It could be twenty minutes, might be a couple hours. I doubt it's been that long since we're still driving."

Christa's voice was muffled meaning she probably had a bag over her head too.

Sloane tried to sit up but couldn't manage it. Instead she listened, hoping to hear a sound from outside the vehicle to tell her where she was because anything might be a clue. But it was quiet. Not the tinkle of a slot machine through an open casino door downtown, the honk another car at a stoplight, nor music from a live band could be heard if they were still in the hustle bustle of downtown. The world outside was silent. Plus, she rolled at every turn, either into the side of the vehicle or into Christa. She tried counting the turns but gave up trying to figure out where they were taking her after the fifth right turn.

It felt like they were going in circles. The sack over

her head made it hard to breathe. There was plenty of oxygen coming though the tiny holes, but it was hot inside and smelled like mothballs.

It seemed like they drove forever, but she was convinced from the number of right turns they were taking, they weren't actually going as far as the men driving wanted them to think. If they were heading out into the desert, they would have gotten on the freeway and taken it out of town.

Finally, the vehicle came to a halt and the engine shut down.

"Get up," Christa ordered, nudging her with a shoulder. "On your feet."

She struggled to obey, but managed to make it to her knees, then her feet using the side of the truck as a crutch. Straining her ears, she listened for any hint of voices telling her where they were, but there was only the sound of marching footsteps before the door creaked open.

"All right, ladies, let's go."

Sloane was hefted over someone's shoulder. From the grunt she heard, Christa was receiving the same treatment. Her stomach rolled, objecting to the pounding it received with every step. The man held her legs with one of his arms and with her arms tied behind her back and her head covered, there wasn't much else she could do. She couldn't even bite him. She was helpless, which made her mad.

Super-stinking mad.

A door swung open and she could hear other voices. Deep, male voices talking and laughing casually, as if this was day to day routine to them.

"Where does the boss want these two?" a baritone

voice as smooth as cream asked from beside her head.

"Take the slutty looking one to room twelve. The other one comes with me." This man's voice was higher pitched and weaselly.

Slutty looking one? She didn't know if that was her or Christa since she was still wearing Christa's dress. She also didn't know if she wanted it to be her. Was room twelve a better option? Her heart pounded and her breath started coming in sharp gasps. She was beginning to panic again, which wasn't good. She struggled to keep it from overwhelming her, needing to be prepared for whatever happened next.

She was carried into the building and straight down a hall. The voices diminishing with every thudding step the man carrying her took. She was alone with him, whoever he was. She clenched her hands where they were tied, anger fighting against her panic. To calm herself, she focused on keeping track of where she was in the building. Left then right. Left again. When the brute finally came to a halt, her hips were bruised, and her legs felt like jelly. She bent her knees a few times, trying to get the blood flowing again.

She heard the sound of a door opening, the hinges in need of some oil, then a gravelly voice called, "Who's there." It was too quiet to tell if it was Jonah or not, but her ears perked up, listening for more.

"Have fun, toots." The weaselly man hissed loudly in her ear. It tickled her eardrum and she raised her shoulder on instinct, knocking his chin away. In retaliation, he tossed her to the floor, her face slamming into the dirt. The dust filtered through the tiny holes in the burlap sack, filling her mouth and making her want to sneeze. A thud next to her told her something else was tossed in behind her. Then a heavy door banged shut and she heard a sharp *snick* as the bolt slid into the place on the other side.

Reaching on the ground, she felt around with her hands until she found what they'd thrown in after her. Surprisingly, it was the knife again. She'd forgotten about it when they were in the van.

The moment her hand touched it, the sharp pain returned to her back as if she was being stabbed repeatedly at the base of her spine. Gritting her teeth, she used her bound hands to pick it up, flipping it over by feel and cutting her fingers in the process. The blade was sharp. She knew it was the same knife from Xavier's collection with the rubies on the hilt. The jewels dug into her palms as she held it between them, sawing at the rope. After a little while, she was able to free her hands. Next, she snapped the twine around her neck and lifted off her burlap sack to see where she was and froze.

It was *the room.*

As in the room from the videos playing at Xavier's.

Dim lights were flickering on the walls and while she cut her feet free, she realized the knife she held was simply beautiful. It had a long thin blade and a dozen rubies surrounded by diamonds worked into its golden hilt.

She heard a groan from across the room and looked up, seeing the man from the monitors. Head sagging inside the sack, arms and legs still bound.

"Jonah?" she whispered, half terrified it would be some aberration of the man she loved under the burlap bag.

"Sloane?"

The voice was Jonah's but, at the same time, it wasn't. It was a growl. A hiss. A deep, dark desire in his voice that haunted her and would for the rest of her days.

"It's me, don't worry. I'm here. I'll get you free." She stood on shaky legs, stumbling across the dirt floor to reach the chair where he was tied. Reaching up, she went to remove the sack from his head, but he thrashed in the seat, pulling away from her. "Don't!" he yelled. "We can't stop them. We have to keep them apart."

She had no idea what he was talking about and she didn't care. He must be delirious. Taking up her ruby-handled blade, she snapped the tie and pulled off the sack.

It really was him! He was alive and well. All she could think was that at least they were together now. They could deal with anything together.

Looking up, she found the video camera in the corner, the red light telling her it was on and active. She'd almost forgotten they weren't alone. She flipped it the bird before turning back to Jonah.

"Oh, god. Hold on, I'll get you free." She went to press her lips against his, but he squeezed his eyes shut and spit in her face.

Squinching her face in disgust, she wiped at her eyes with her hands.

"What the hell did you do that for, you idiot?" she demanded. "I'm trying to help you."

"You aren't real. You aren't her," he yelled, his voice loud in the small room.

"Of course, it's me. Who else would be dumb enough to get caught while trying to save you. I'll admit, I look a bit fancier than normal in this get-up, but it was just my disguise to get in here and save you. Hold still so I can get you untied."

He began to buck wildly against the ropes holding him, making it impossible for her to cut him free. "I said STOP!"

She leaned back, sagging until she sat cross-legged on the floor and looked up at his tortured face. "What are you talking about? We have to get out of here."

With a deep sigh, he shook his head. "Neither one of us is meant to get out of here. Not alive anyway." His eyes fixated on the object on the table in front of him. "If you untie me, we'll kill each other."

She stood slowly, her own hand moving inextricably closer to the…was it another…knife?

When she got a few inches from it, she arched her back and screamed. She'd been stabbed again! She was sure of it this time. She had one knife in her hand and the other was on the table so there must be another one in the room. One that was now protruding from her back. Wheeling around in circles, she looked for the offending object, swatting with her own knife. "How did you stab me when you're tied up? Seriously, why would you do that, Jonah? I didn't stab you! Get it out! Get it out!"

He lifted his head, his eyes hooded. "You get used to the pain. It'll move around. And there's only one cure. These are the Twin Blades of Butchery. They want blood. Ours. And not just a couple of drops from your hands. The deep pumping blood of a vein that fuels life into our hearts."

Dropping her ruby knife on the ground, she stepped away and skidded backwards until she hit the wall. Wrapping her arms around her legs, she hugged herself tight. With the knives in the same room together, she didn't need Jonah to spell it all out for her. She could feel their painful calling deep in her soul.

The call for love. The call for hate.

Now she understood the pain in Angus Finch's eyes when he'd spoke about them at the panel that afternoon.

The knives pulled at her emotions, making them stronger. Making her burn. She turned toward Jonah, her panic spiking as their eyes met. In spite of everything going on around them, she ached for him, ached for him like no pain she had ever known.

She wanted to rip his hair out with her teeth, inhale his skin in bites, and ravage him until the next century. The love she felt for him became carnal, unfulfilled lust and her palms began to sweat. Her body started to tremble, like a drug addict too long without a fix.

Even his ragged breathing was making her hot, her nipples hardened, and an ache began within her. She dared not look at him for fear she would keep him tied up and have her way with him. Over and over in an endless loop of everlasting satisfaction.

"What are we supposed to do now?" she croaked, imagining climbing into his lap as he sat in the chair, the feel of his hardness beneath her.

But no. That's what the blades wanted. She needed to focus. To keep her distance. There was no denying this now they were in the same room together with the knives. She could feel them pulling at her, forcing her closer to him. Without realizing what she was doing, she moved closer to him, her body compelled to touch him, feel the heat of him against her as they came together.

"I don't understand what's going on?" she stopped walking, shaking her head to clear it.

"Do you know about the blades?" he asked.

She nodded remembering what Angus Finch said. "They have something to do with lovers."

"Not 'something', but everything to do with love. I tried to keep the information from them but somehow, they found out. They could put anyone besides you in this room with me and though we'd be in pain from the stabbing sensations, the blades would not ask for the ultimate sacrifice. But now that they brought you here, there's nothing we can do to fight it."

"Is this your round-a-bout way of saying 'I love you?'" Sloane laughed. "And because of that the knives will make us kill each other? You really know how to show a girl a good time. Instead of dragging me here and having a fight to the death to show you love me, you could've just called."

For some reason, the thought of dying wasn't bothering her. Other things were more important, like the way her body sizzled when she was near him, coming to life. Oh, and then there was the other thing…

Her eyes strayed to the growing bulge in his lap. The lap she wanted to…

Focus. She needed to focus. She shifted her eyes to his face but that wasn't much better. His lips looked soft and kissable as they lifted into a half smile.

"But what if I don't love you back? What if my heart really still belongs to Michael? I've never said it to you, have I? Could that save us?" she asked.

"Is that true?" he asked.

He looked at her through lowered lashes and her heart skipped a beat. She couldn't lie to him. Not even to save their lives. Especially since the blades would know and she doubted Xavier would believe her anyway.

"No. It's not. I love you. It sounds cliché but I think, in a way, I've always loved you," she told him. "But, right now that's bad, isn't it? What are we going to do?"

"Come over here and find out." His voice was husky. There was no masking his deep-seeded desire for her and she liked it. Wanted more. Licking her lips, she crawled on all fours toward him. Then under the table. With her hands she untied his feet and with her mouth she bit at the hardness between his legs through his pants. He moaned.

As soon as his legs were free, she found them wrapped around her middle and he fell on the floor. The instant he lessened his vice grip, she snaked her way up to his mouth, unbuttoning his shirt and kissing and nipping her way along his abdomen coming even closer to the prize still hidden below. He arched when she crawled over his pelvis and she kissed him hard, forcibly. Her need for every ounce of him overrode every other emotion. He was to be hers. And only hers. Forever.

His eyes were barely open, and his look told her what she already knew. They couldn't fight this. She didn't even want to.

She worked her way forward and ripped open the bodice of her dress to expose herself to him. He bit down hard on her nipple sending a shiver of pleasure through her entire being. In the back of her mind, she felt a twinge of unease. There was a reason she shouldn't be doing this and not just because of the knives. Something about a camera…but she was too far gone to stop.

Not caring about the consequences, she worked at his hands. She needed those free. To touch her, caress her, love her. As soon as his hands were free, one was around her neck. His eyes were black, and he slapped her hard, the two of them toppling onto the dirt floor.

"You fucked him, didn't you?"

Choking, she shook her head. "Who?"

"Xavier." He spat.

"Never," she managed to get the words out.

He released her and rolled on his back.

Jumping to her feet, rage now overtook her. "You're the one who's been with that slut partner of yours." Wheeling around, she lunged for her ruby knife she'd dropped on the floor after cutting him loose and threw it at his face. He sidestepped, and the knife stuck in the wall behind him.

"Really?" He laughed, his eyes wild and not his own. He reached for the sapphire knife on the table, palming it in his hand. "That's how you're going to play it? I see you. All dolled up, tossed in here like the sloppy seconds you are. Xavier and his boys already had their turns on you, and I'll bet you loved it."

The rage growing inside of her was what blurred the line between the most intense love and the most insane jealousy and hatred. They fed off one another until she felt like she would burst. Her jealousy was fueled by her love and her love empowered her rage.

Her yin yang of sadistic lust and unquenchable rage boiled in her blood like molten lava waiting to explode and destroy the mountainside. Every cell in her body hummed.

Never had she felt more teeming with life and ready to pounce on her prey like a mountain lion. Sliding her back against the wall, she edged her way to the ruby knife.

"You are forgetting who left who, my love," she told him. "One night of pleasure with me and it was back to hiding out with your sex crazed partner. Well, this little unwholesome threesome does not have my consent. When you mount Christa in the morning, that gives you no right to send me a quiet love-text of goodnight.

"I hate your dirty thoughts of having us both in your bed. If I can't have you all to myself, I'll make sure no one has you." Her voice dropped an octave as she spoke, becoming more sinister and chilling. The words came out though she wasn't sure if she really meant them. Didn't she love him? Still she said it and it felt real.

Deep in her heart she knew what she was saying wasn't true. None of this was. Not the things he was saying about her or her wild accusations. But she couldn't stop them from pouring from her mouth any more than she could stop reaching for him. Wanting him.

Her groping hand found the ruby handled knife and she extracted it from the wall as they continued in their dangerous dance.

He threw his head back in laughter and lifted his lip in a sneer. "You think you have it bad because Christa is my partner? It's not like you're the one who had to listen to his best friend, Michael, tell the moaning tales of pleasure with the only woman *I've* ever wanted. I'm the one who had to endure that. In fact, I'm glad he's dead!" he yelled, hitting his breastbone with the hand not clutching the knife. His fist made a dull thud against his skin. "You have no idea of that pain, but I'll help you understand the true meaning of physical pain."

His words made her insides ripple like waves crashing to shore on a rough sea. The palms of her hands were moist with sweat, making her move the knife between them so she could wipe off the offending palm. She ached for the pain he'd give her. Ached for the tension. The surrender. The release.

"Michael was my gateway drug to get to you. Come and get me, I'm all yours." She sank to her knees, closing her eyes and throwing her head back, inviting him to her. Inviting everything he embodied in her disheveled brain: the weight of his body on hers, the scent of his lust commingled with hers, his feverish touch and the perfect way they fit together as a man and woman.

The dirt floor crunched as he rushed at her, tackling her to the ground. "I'm so sorry. I didn't mean that," he whispered in her ear in a fractional moment of lucidity. The second she opened her eyes and locked on his, the hysteria was back in torrents, the sprinkle of rain turned to a full-on thunderstorm.

They wrestled, rolling over again and again, each trying to get the better vantage. His strength seemed underwhelming to her. Random thoughts fizzled in her brain and broke through the intensity: *Why was he so weak? How long had he been here? Was he letting her win? Why couldn't she stop herself?*

Panting, he paused for a moment on his back and she held the knife to his throat, not recognizing her own hand or its gravitational movement to overcome and vanquish her opponent. Her movements were not her own. Her body was not under her control and her brain had entirely succumbed to the lure of the Twin Blades. A fragmental piece of her spared psyche was on pins and needles, pushed into a small windowless room with no hope of escape. Waiting for the inevitable.

"Do it, then. Take what you need. Do what must be done," Jonah closed his eyes and spread his arms out to his sides, the hand with the knife convulsing like it was a struggling living puppet in the hands of an inexperienced puppeteer, fighting its master for control of its own destiny.

She didn't need him to ask twice. Holding the knife between her teeth, she unbuckled his pants and pulled them to his knees, before slicing at the fabric of her gown until she'd ripped the skirt away, then the undergarments beneath. Reaching with one hand he stroked his shaft as he waited for her to ready herself. She slapped his hand away, flinging the skirt aside as she climbed on top of him.

He moaned and cried out her name, gritting his teeth and refusing to open his eyes. She descended into a drug-like ecstasy letting all sensations pierce her as she rocked back and forth in a hypnotic rhythm.

She froze, knowing the slightest movement would tumble forward a release on both their parts. "Don't you dare finish," she warned.

His whole body began to convulse from the stalemate and in that slightest movement, she lost her final hold on sanity. Lifting the ruby-encrusted knife over her head in both hands, she vowed in her psychotic brain that no other woman would ever have him again.

"I love you, too much." Her voice was not her own and they both shook in passionate release. He opened his eyes watching her without fear or hatred, but a tinge of sadness, as he watched the knife in her hand descending toward his chest.

At the last minute, her brain seemed to catch up with what her body was doing. She saw the lights glint off the sharp silver blade and gasped, trying to stop herself. Because of her hesitation, the blade missed her target and plunged into the upper right side of his chest, its ruby hilt protruding from his body.

As soon as her fingers released the haunted knife, all Jonah's thoughts flooded into her senses. She could hear him saying things like: *I forgive you. You don't know what you're doing. You don't mean what you're saying. If you can hear me Sloane, get ready…*

She looked at him quizzically, like he'd said the words out loud. Seeing him like this was surreal, like she was watching a movie. But certainly, this wasn't a movie set, and she didn't play an actress' leading role. Plus, the blood pooling out around the blade still sticking out of his chest, wasn't fake.

He threw her off of him, snatching up his own discarded blade lying in the dust beside them.

"Get ready," he panted. "You can run."

"I'm sorry," she whispered, not understanding his words as she focused on the knife lodged in his chest. The knife she had put there.

"It's ok…not your fault…there's more going on here than…"

Just then, the door to the room flung open and Christa bolted inside, rushing to Jonah's side. "What have you done?" Christa wailed, reaching for the knife to remove it when Sloane heard a bang so loud, all she heard afterward was a humming sound deep in her ears.

Standing beside her, Jonah dropped to his knees before falling face first to the floor.

"Jonah!" She screamed, dropping to the ground next to him and rolling him onto his back. The knife had slid deeper, its hilt disappearing beneath his skin. She ran her hands over his chest, looking for the bullet hole but she couldn't find it. There was so much blood. Some of it was from the knife but there had to be a bullet hole. She just couldn't find it. "Ohmigod. Ohmigod. What happened? What's going on?"

"I didn't shoot him, obviously. There's no need after what you did, but I can't have the two of you trying to save him. That would go against everything I've worked so hard to orchestrate."

She searched for the source of the voice and found Xavier looming in the doorway like the two-legged monster he was. He sauntered into the room, a smile on his lips and a gun held loosely in one hand, its muzzle pointed toward the ceiling. From his demeanor, Sloane realized he'd shot at the ceiling, not at Jonah.

"Nicely played, my dear. Once your Romeo takes his last breath, this film will be worth something."

Following his eyes to the wall, she was reminded of the camera which had filmed the whole thing. The same video feed she had first seen Jonah on in the hotel room had recorded everything they'd done. She'd seen it when she first entered the room and completely forgot about its silent presence after that.

She felt blood rushing to her cheeks and a roar in her ears. Sick to her stomach, she forced herself to take several deep breaths before she vomited on the floor in front of Xavier. They'd already gotten a video of her having sex and now they were going to let Jonah die.

"You won't get away with this!" she screamed. "And he's not going to die. I won't let him!"

"I will get away with it," Xavier said calmly, raising the gun to point at her. "After all, most people don't recover from a knife to the chest. You, my dear, have just murdered an FBI agent. Now get away from him before I decide to shoot you. Your pretty face could fetch a price in the right markets."

"Get off of him. Let me see if I can help!" Christa screamed, pushing at Sloane.

"Don't touch him," Sloane said, covering him with her chest so she was practically lying on top of him. "Jonah, you can't die. You can't."

Tears were streaming down her cheeks, but she didn't wipe them away. She clung to him like he was all that was holding her to this world because, well, that was closer to the truth than she usually wanted to admit.

"Seriously, Sloane, move," Christa grabbed her hair, pulling until she was forced to sit up. "I have emergency medic training. Let me look at him."

Glancing at Jonah, Sloane saw his eyes on her. He lay still, pain contorting his features. He lifted one hand, his fingers softly wiping the tears from her eye before caressing her cheek.

She heard his voice in her head loud and clear: *"Go. Run,"* as he pressed the sapphire blade into her palm with his other hand. And she understood. In his last breaths, all he cared about was her safety and getting her out of there.

With a sob, she sat up, allowing Christa to move into the space she'd just vacated. The blonde nudged her with her shoulder, demanding more room and Sloane stood, glancing toward the open door.

She knew she should listen to Jonah and run but how could she leave him here to die? Christa reached up from where she was leaning over Jonah, grabbing her by what was left of her dress and pulling her down next to her. She bent awkwardly, her head next to Christa's mouth.

"Run. I've got this." Christa whispered before letting her go.

Should she go? Could she trust Christa to step up to the plate and save Jonah? Slowly, so she wouldn't attract attention to her, she slid one step toward the open door.

Xavier took deliberate steps toward Jonah, pointing the gun at Christa. "Leave him. He needs to die."

"I will not. You'll have to put a bullet in my head to get me to stop," Christa spat.

"I'm serious, slut. He needs to die." Xavier stepped forward, putting the muzzle of the gun directly against the side of her head. "You may think I don't know who you are, but I know all about you and your FBI connections. You're lucky, because of them you're still of use to me. Otherwise, I'd have no problem putting a hole in you."

Christa flinched as if he'd struck her, but the fire quickly returned to her eyes as she faced off against Xavier, pulling his attention to her.

Sloane concealed the knife in what was left of her skirt as she continued a slow sidestep to the open door when Jonah lifted his head and nodded at her. She heard him in her head though his voice sounding weak and tinny, as if he was getting further away.

Now, Go now. Run. Don't stop and don't come back.

It happened so fast, she almost missed it as she slipped through the door. Christa reached up, grabbing Xavier's wrist and twisting. The gun went off, but she was already running down the hall, retracing what she remembered of the turns.

She heard another shot. Had Jonah been shot? Or what if Christa was the one hit? Should she go back and try to help or run like Jonah told her?

She slowed, her heart pounding and breath came in sharp gasps.

Her indecision saved her life.

A loud shot and a bullet whizzed by her ear, slamming into the wall in front of her. She took off again, heading for the exit as she heard another bullet fire and Christa screaming. A loud, long scream like the sound of someone's soul being ripped through their throat as their heart pumps their last.

Was she dead too? She didn't know.

She wanted to turn back, but she couldn't make herself do it. Jonah had told her to run.

Jonah. Had Xavier killed Jonah? Had one of those gunshots finished him off?

But did that really matter? She'd stabbed him before the gunshots.

His death would forever be on her hands.

But he couldn't be dead, could he? She'd know if he was dead. She'd feel it somehow because they were connected, wouldn't she? She didn't know anymore.

Trying not to sob, she rocketed through a steel door into the cool Nevada night. She was in a warehouse, not a cave. The bastard had just wanted it to look like a cave.

The moon was full and with its light she could see a conversion van parked nearby. Like a gift, it was unlocked, and the key was still in the ignition. Stupid henchmen probably didn't think there was a chance she'd get away. How wrong they were.

Grabbing a long-sleeved jacket tossed on the passenger seat, she zipped it up to cover herself the best she could, turned the key, revved the engine and sped off onto the lonely desert road.

Chapter 9

The only bit of good news was she had been right. They hadn't gone far. The lights of the Vegas Strip sparkled in the distance. The bastards really had driven in circles while she and Christa were stuck in the back of the van with their heads covered to confuse them.

At least it made her life easier. She wasn't in any shape to make major decisions at the moment. The empty highway outside the warehouse gave her two options. She could head into the darkness where desert hills rose like burial mounds threatening to swallow her whole, or toward the bright lights of the city.

The lights it was.

She knew she should go to the police but was afraid to try to explain what happened. Especially considering she was wearing a coat, a ripped dress and no underwear. Not to mention she didn't even really know what happened. Was Jonah dead. Holding back a sob, she accepted he probably was. What if they sent her to jail for killing Jonah? He was an FBI agent. They had the death penalty in Nevada. She was a coward and didn't want to die. But what should she do besides drive toward the lights in the distance?

Leaving her dismal failure behind her, she focused on trying to obey Jonah's words. All that mattered was getting away. Doing something to keep herself from focusing on what had just happened.

Every time she squeezed the steering wheel, a sharp pain tore through her palm. She must have been injured and didn't realize it. Injured she could handle. At least she wasn't dead like…

She couldn't think about that right now.

Ignoring the pain in her left hand, she pushed on the accelerator, going as fast as she could. She needed to figure out where to go. Where would she be safe? She needed a place Xavier and his goons would never think to look for her.

For some reason, the strange jingle Angus Finch had used at the panel kept swirling through her head, like the most annoying earworm in the history of songs you can't get out of your brain. She could even hear him singing it in his off-key voice.

If you want a good scare while you're in town, try Finch's House on Fourth and Crown.

Pulling up to a red light, she glanced up at the street sign. That was it. She needed to go to Finch. Not only would Xavier and his men never expect her to go there but Finch had owned the knives so he might be able to tell her what had just happened.

Unbidden, the image of Jonah's face flashed before her eyes but not the smiling, loving man she was used to. It was the snarling, angry man she'd actually stabbed with a knife.

Stifling a sob, she gunned the engine as the light turned green, the wheel ripping into her hand again. She couldn't think about what happened now. She needed to get somewhere safe and fast.

Only she had no idea where she was or which direction to head in.

When she got to the city, she avoided the Strip and

drove aimlessly, trying to find either fourth street or Crown. She really wished she had her phone and could get the lady on Google to give her directions, but Xavier's men had taken it. After zigzagging across the side streets, she gave up just before reaching the airport and pulled into the drive-thru line at a 24-hour fast food place to get directions.

The boy behind the little glass window looked frightened when she pulled up and she understood. After all, she was driving a creepy van and she knew there was dirt and tear stains on her face, Her feet were bare, and her hair probably looked like she was Medusa's little sister. And to top it all off, she was half naked and covered in blood.

But she must have looked as bad as she felt because he took pity on her and gave her the directions she needed. Good thing he did too because she was on the complete wrong end of town.

She quickly made her way to Finch's place. It was easy to spot. The brick building was squashed between two equally run-down wooden stores—one a pawn shop, the other a salon with a sign reading "Karen for Yer Hair" in the window. A moldy faded red awning hung over the storefront window with a display of creepy looking porcelain dolls, a planchette from a Ouija board, and a few of what could have been Native American or even Mayan idols.

She drove around the block, taking the alley behind the store. She was relieved when she saw it had an upstairs apartment attached. Even though it was very late—or early—there was a chance Angus lived there and would be home this time of night. Sloane wasn't even sure what time it was, but midnight had to be long gone by now.

Taking the steep wooden stairs two at a time, she rapped the knuckles of her right hand on the door frantically as soon as she reached it while searching for a bell. Frustrated she couldn't find one, she knocked harder. This whole thing felt like some B-rated zombie or horror movie and she wanted out. She felt a sob building in her chest and bit her lip to keep from releasing it. She was near her breaking point.

But then, it hadn't been the best day. Actually, it had been a tie for the worst day in her life. She'd been coerced from her amazing hotel room in St. Louis, in the middle of a bubble bath, and put on a plane. She'd flown to Las Vegas only to be primped and prodded by Jonah's bitch of a partner, who wasn't actually as bad as she'd thought, done a panel, gone to a ball, been kidnapped, thrown into a dungeon-like chamber, been the main attraction for a bunch of voyeurs, and she'd killed her best friend/lover by stabbing him.

Jonah.

Jonah was dead.

She clenched her teeth together until her jaw hurt, trying to keep the tears from falling. They burned the back of her eyes and she felt a sob build in her throat.

No, she refused to believe it. She'd injured him, maybe. And he was still breathing after she ran. Or maybe this was all a surreal nightmare and she'd wake up soon covered in sweat padding to her kitchen for a glass of lifesaving water. That was the best hope. But how to wake up from this nightmare?

She knocked again, leaning her head against the warped wood on the door and trying to keep the front of her jacket closed. All she needed now was to be arrested for indecent exposure.

"Please be home," she whispered as she pounded her fist on the wood. "Please, please, please."

The inner door creaked open, almost making her stumble, and revealing one eye peeking out below the chain lock.

"Mr. Finch," Sloane gasped, straightening. "Please, I need help."

"Sloane?" Angus pushed the door shut and she heard him fumble with the chain before pulling it open. He glanced at her, his heading dipping as he took her in from head to toe and she tried not to grimace. She knew what he saw. His eyes widened and fear crept into his gaze.

"I'm sorry to come by so late but I didn't know where else to go."

"You're in trouble." It wasn't a question.

"I was kidnapped by Mr. X. The man who owns the hotel," she tried to explain. "And he took me somewhere…"

"That's not what I mean," he snapped. "Get in here."

He pulled her into the stairway, locking the door carefully behind him before leading her up some rickety wooden stairs to his apartment. The entry had probably been painted white at one time but was now a dingy sort of gray with cobwebs dusting the corners and dirt caked on the linoleum floor.

"Thank you," Sloane breathed, feeling safe for the moment as she trudged into his kitchen. It was small, with just a few feet of counter next to a sink and an old, yellow fridge. There wasn't even a stove, just a hot plate and a microwave but it looked enormously safer than Xavier's fortieth floor suite. "Do you think I could have some water?"

Finch ignored her, heading straight to the counter and fumbling through the drawers until he came out with a large plastic bag and a tub of table salt. Snapping open the bag, he dumped the entire container of salt into it.

"Put it in here," he said, closing his eyes and holding out the bag as if he couldn't bear to look at her. "Quickly."

"Put what in there?" she asked.

He gestured to her hand with an audible gulp that told her he was afraid. She looked down and gasped. Clutched in her left hand was the knife. Part of the hilt stuck out by her pinky, showing off the sapphires, while the wavy tip stuck out near her thumb. Blood dripped from where blade had slid into her grip and sliced into her palm and her fingers during her drive here. Somehow, she'd kept a hold of it while fleeing for her life.

"Nonononono!" she cried, trying to hand the blade to Angus, but the old man backed away, holding out the plastic bag.

"Put it in here. And, for the love of all things holy, don't touch me with it," he said, and his harsh words broke through her panic. "It can't stay here but I know someone who can deal with it."

He held the bag open wide and she dropped the knife inside, prying her fingers off one by one, drops of her blood coating the salt and turning it red. Finally, the blade slipped free, resting on top of the salt. He zipped the top tight and shook the bag a few times, making sure the whole knife was covered before turning to her.

"Stay here," he told her, as if she had somewhere to go.

He left through a side door.

Sloane didn't know where he'd gone but could hear him rummaging around in another room. At least he hadn't left. Her hands shaking, she grabbed a glass off the counter with her non-bloody hand, filling it at the sink and draining the water in seconds. She filled it again and was just taking a drink when he returned, clutching a pair of old sweats and a plain gray t-shirt in his hands.

"Sorry, I really needed a drink," she said.

"No worries. Here, put this on." He turned his back so she could get them on.

"Where did you get that knife?" he asked when she was decent.

"I don't know. They gave it to me," Sloane replied.

"Who's they?" he asked, pulling her over to the sink and rinsing her hand with warm water before wrapping it in a length of white bandage.

"I don't know. Mr. X and his men. The ones who kidnapped me and Christa. Oh, god, Christa! I just left her there. I left Christa behind. I killed Jonah and I left her behind to be tortured and killed!"

She saw black dots swirl in front of her eyes and knew she was going to pass out.

He grabbed her by the arm, tugging her into his living room, before pushing her down on the couch and forcing her head between her knees.

"You're in shock," he said, gently patting the top of her head in a completely unhelpful and annoying way. "Just relax. We'll figure this out. I don't think it's a coincidence the knife you brought here was one of the knives I was questioned about at the panel. I always knew it would find its way back to me after what happened. I tried to keep them apart, but they always seek out their mate. We don't have much time, please tell me everything. From the beginning."

"The Twin Blades of Butchery," she nodded, looking up at him sideways while keeping her head between her knees until the black spots faded. "So they are real. And damn haunted, let me tell you."

Feeling a slight bit better, she sat up. She heard an odd cooing sound and looked around, spotting an old TV and a pile of books on the coffee table before she saw a birdcage hanging near his front window housing what looking like a pigeon. Something was even attached to his leg like an old carrier pigeon from World War II. Everything happening was so weird, she didn't even question. It made sense Angus would have a carrier pigeon. Why not?

"You brought back the sapphire blade," Finch said. "I would know it anywhere. And you don't have to tell me they are cursed. I already know all about them." His eyes were haunted as if he was reliving a painful memory by being close to the blade. "If anyone knows how dangerous those knives are, it's me."

"But if it's all true, then I really did…" Her face must have lost all its color again because the old man jumped toward her with a muttered oath, easing her head back down between her knees and holding her there until her breathing was steady again.

"I think you need to tell me everything," Angus said, taking a seat beside her on the couch and taking her hand in his.

Her first instinct was to pull away, but it wasn't a

disgustingly clingy gesture like Alvin Mitchell would have done. Alvin had tried to kill her, but she didn't feel like Angus was anything like him. This was more comforting. He patted their joined hands with his other, looking uncomfortable and a little confused. It was nice. Like a grandfather who was there to look out for her, so she held on to his hand as she told him everything that happened since the panel ended.

She didn't leave anything out, going from the invitation to Mr. X's penthouse to when he'd abducted Christa and her and driven them to a warehouse. She slowed, not wanting to get into all the details of what happened when she'd been thrown in the room with Jonah and each of them given a knife.

"It's ok," he said, nodding with a sad smile on his weathered face. "I understand. It was the same with my wife."

"Your wife?" she asked, wiping away a tear from her cheek before it could fall.

"My Martha. I loved that woman to death, literally," he said "She knew, right at the end, the blades had control of us. Rather than kill me, she took her own life. She loved me that much.

There's such a fine line between love and hate, though, isn't there? They're opposite emotions and they're so strong, one can quickly turn into the other in the heat of a moment. Those blades were cast to bring all of that to light."

She nodded. That was exactly what she'd been feeling. She loved Jonah so much she hated him. Or maybe it was the other way around?

"Did it feel like they stabbed you in the back when they gave you the knife?" Finch asked.

"No, they actually did…" she reached back, expecting to find a wound in her lower back but there wasn't anything there.

"My pain diminished in the years after the knives were stolen," he said. "I think it's their way of marking us with their curse. I still feel a twinge of pain every now and again, as if they're reminding me I live on borrowed time."

"Borrowed time?"

"The blades want blood. They've almost always been found with a couple thought to be deeply in love. Usually one of them was dead," Finch explained. "The knives want true love's blood to flow." His pained look returned. "When my wife died, only one of the blades succeeded. I buried the blades in the middle of a forest, but someone found them. Someone always finds them. Their call for blood is too strong."

"Then I killed him," she let her face sink into her hands and began to sob.

"There, there," he patted her shoulder, a worried crease on his brow and his voice cracked a little as if he, too, felt her pain. "I wish I could tell you differently, but in my experience, no one person can fight the blades' powerful desires when they are seeking blood."

She closed her eyes, taking a deep breath through her nose and trying to settle her spirit the way Stephanie had taught her. But there would be no settling this pain. Ever.

Stephanie!

She needed to talk with her. Stephanie might know how to sever the blades' connection but there's no way she could ever face her again. Not after what she'd done to Jonah.

"Could I borrow your phone?" she asked Angus. "I need to call New York."

"You'll have to do it collect. I have a landline down in the museum for customer calls," he said, gesturing to a set of stairs leading down toward the front of the shop. "I only have one down there because I have to. They're always watching, you know, and listening. It's not safe to have one of those portable phones on you at all times."

She didn't even want to ask who *"they"* were. He was obviously paranoid about outsiders. "Thanks, I'll just be a minute."

The stairs led down into the museum on the main floor. A sign hung on the door to the museum. "Should something happen to me, release the bird.—Angus Finch" What would it be like to be so old and eccentric you didn't even have a cell phone, let alone a landline in your apartment? Not to mention sending messages via carrier pigeon? She didn't really want to know.

The place was creepy in an intentional way. Not only was there a mass of haunted objects scattered and piled half-hazardly around the room, it was an interior designer's nightmare.

The walls were covered with a dark brown wooden paneling and the orange shag carpet on the floor could only have been from the 1970s. The curtains a yellow floral pattern from the 1950s, which may have been the last time the place was dusted as well. Spider webs clung to every surface, sweeping from beaded lampshades to antique furniture. The corners were masses of lacy artwork where years of dust stuck to the webs making them sag with their own weight.

Even though the museum was completely different from Xavier's fancy jewelry store-esque way of storing his items, they were roughly the same. Angus had amassed a bizarre collection of jewelry, toys, children's dolls, old farm implements, a few gowns, and even some wooden boxes.

One glass cabinet stood in the corner with a large note on the door reading: *Do not look in mirror! Has been involved in at least one murder. Believed to be possessed by a demon claiming to be the ghost of a child.*

Inside was a small oval hand mirror with a short pewter handle, parts of it spotted brown with age. For a moment, Sloane felt a pull, like a call, demanding she check her reflection in the shining surface, but she hurriedly turned away. She'd had enough of haunted items.

Picking up the heavy black handset, she held it to her ear listening to a sound she hadn't heard in years. A dial tone.

The phone was rotary, because why would someone like Angus Finch actually have a phone with a keypad? Instead of trying to dial, she stuck her finger in the hole for the zero and slid it around, hoping there were still people out there who worked as operators at all hours of the day and night.

Right away she was rewarded.

"Operator," the woman's voice twanged through the line.

"I'd like to make a collect call to New York," Sloane said, giving the woman the number for Aunt Steph's cell phone.

The phone had barely rung when Steph picked up.

"Thank the goddess, it's you," Steph practically shouted through the line. "I've been trying to get through to you, but you haven't been answering your phone."

"I don't have it. I was kidnapped. Listen, Steph, I have to tell you something important."

"No, I have to tell you something important. So important I'm going to ignore the kidnapped comment for a moment."

She clenched her free hand at her side, closing her eyes and forcing the words past the lump in her throat.

"Steph, I have to tell you this. I think I killed Jonah. Or if I didn't, I caused his death."

There. She'd said it. He was dead because of her.

"I don't believe you. My Jonie is just fine, you wait and see. You're the one in trouble. I can't tell where you are right now, but there's someone there. You need to get out. Leave now. I was wrong about who to trust. You didn't meet him until later. And though you've seen him, he's not with you now. He's close though and he can help. You need…"

The sound of breaking glass followed by a loud thud from above made her jerk her head away from the headset to look up. Suddenly she was filled with dread.

"I have to go, Steph. I'll call you soon."

"Wait! No, you have to hear this. Don't trust…"

She dropped the handset, running for the stairs. She hit the living room at a sprint, skidding to a stop. A window stood ajar and the door to the birdcage was open, blood on the hinge as if Angus had crawled to it. He was lying on the floor next to the cage, a growing pool of blood surrounding him. The sapphire knife stuck out of his chest at an odd angle, like whoever had stabbed him had known just how to hold the knife to get past the ribs and do the most damage. His whole chest was a series of wounds, the blood draining down his side onto the floor.

"No!" she cried, running to his side.

"He's…coming…" he wheezed, arching his back in pain. Blood leaked from the side of his mouth.

Sloane reached for the sapphire handle, intending to remove it, but the knife stuck, refusing to move.

"Who's coming?" she asked, taking his hand in her own and clutching it to her chest, half expecting Xavier to push through the kitchen door and kill her next.

"The past caught up," he said, his voice barely a whisper. Sloane leaned in to hear his words. "Now I'll get to see my Martha again. It's been so long. I hope she loves me enough not to hate me for what happened."

"Oh, Angus, I'm sure she'll understand," she replied, as she finally allowed the tears that had been choking her all night to fall freely from her eyes. "She'll be happy to see you. She'll…"

But his eyes were blank and glassy as they stared beyond her. She held her fingers against his throat, trying again and again in different positions, searching for a pulse. There wasn't one. He was gone. In bringing the knife here, she'd brought his death close at her heels.

Chapter 10

Rocketing back down the stairs, she grabbed the old phone and dialed 9-1-1, irritated at how long it took the nine to spin back to its original position on the rotary dial.

"9-1-1, what's your emergency?" A polite voice asked.

"I'm in Angus Finch's home. He owns the little haunted museum on 4th and Crown. He's been stabbed. I think he's dead. Please send help." She cupped the receiver and looked at a doll in a curio protected under the glass. Had its head turned *toward* her?

"We have your location and help is on the way. Please stay on the phone with me. Can you tell if the subject is breathing?"

"No…he's not. I have to…"

Dropping the phone and letting it dangle, her eyes lingered on the dangerous doll under the glass. It had moved. She was sure of it. She took a step to the side and the doll's head swiveled, following as she moved. With a quick spin, she scanned the room, realizing the place suddenly had a dark, heavy feel over it that hadn't been there before.

It was like a blanket had been draped over everything before to keep others safe. Now the blanket had holes, letting the evil through, and bringing danger too close to the surface. Angus' protective spells cast over the museum were failing.

Backing up to the door step-by-step, the doll's head moved slowly, tracking her every movement. Everything in the room seemed to be watching, an air of malevolent frustration hung in the room. If Angus Finch had died as the result of a curse from a piece of his own collection, what would happen to the rest of it? Acting fast based on Aunt Steph's instructions from the lessons she learned from her from their time together in Maine, she held her arms out wide to cast a protective spell around herself.

Palms facing up, she drew long, deep breaths pulling in divine light through her crown and breathing it out to her fingertips. Her whole body began to buzz from the vibrations she sent forth. Backing up the steps, she locked the museum door and sprinted back upstairs. She kept her eyes straight ahead, not looking at Angus' body as she ran to the kitchen and grabbed the table salt from the counter where he'd left it. Taking it back downstairs she sprinkled the salt along the crack where the stairs meet the door.

Her gaze focused on the sign on the door, "In case of my demise, release the bird.—Angus Finch"

He'd granted his own final wish.

She didn't have time to wonder where the bird would go. Police sirens howled in the neighborhood, getting closer by the minute. She let herself out through the back door, heading down the stairs to the front. She thought about leaving in the van but couldn't.

She knew Angus' death was her fault. She'd brought the knife and it had killed him. Would she spend the rest of her life looking over her shoulder, waiting for the knife to return and kill her too?

Standing out front, she hugged her arms over her chest, not for warmth but comfort. The air outside was hot and dry even though the sun was just beginning to peek over the horizon. Her shirt smelled like Angus—a bit musty and old but covered by laundry detergent. The smell made her want to cry,

The first police car arrived, screeching to a halt in front of the building. Its siren ended mid-whine though the lights were still flashing. A tall, gangly officer with sideburns and mustache that would have been in style in the eighties stepped out of the driver side, hurrying toward her with one hand on the gun holstered at his waist.

"Were you the one who called, Ma'am?" he asked, his mustache wiggling against his lips when he spoke. Two more cruisers arrived with a handful of officers.

"Yes, I called," she told him. "I'm Sloane Osborne."

"I'm Officer DuChien," he said as he pulled a small notebook out of his back pocket, sliding a pencil out from the spiral at the top. He nodded to the officers, indicating they check the building.

"Please use the back door," she called. "The museum isn't safe right now."

"Not safe? Is there someone still inside?" the officer asked.

"Nothing like that. Mr. Finch owned a lot of haunted objects and without his protection spells, it really isn't safe to be near them. I'd recommend calling in a Shaman or a spiritual expert to deal with the items."

"Haunted items? Really?" DuChien said, his eyes narrowing as he jotted a note in the notebook. She could tell he didn't believe her, but he did pass on the order to his men. "Now, Miss Osborne, was it? What is your relationship to Angus Finch?"

"I don't have a relationship with him," she replied, rubbing her hands up and down her arms, not sure why she suddenly felt cold, even in the heat. "I met him today."

"You met him today?" He was jotting something down again. She wished she could tell what he was writing.

Another officer, younger, though still with a toughness about him that spoke of experience, jogged down the alley, returning from behind the museum. He spoke to Officer DuChien in a low tone, but it didn't matter. She knew what he was saying. He was describing Angus and how he looked covered in blood, the jeweled knife sticking out of his chest. DuChien kept looking at her, his expression unreadable.

"Call in forensics," DuChien told the officer in a quiet tone that carried more than the younger man's. "And bag the weapon. We need to get prints. And be sure to check for clues in the museum, haunted objects be damned."

Prints? She wanted to sit down and cry. She'd been holding the knife all night. Which meant her prints were on it. She closed her eyes and shook her head. This wasn't going to look good for her.

"Miss Osborne," Officer DuChien said and she opened her eyes to see the officer heading toward the police cruiser. "I just want to make sure I have this right, you met Mr. Finch today but happened to be in his home tonight when he was murdered?"

She didn't say anything. Just looked at the man.

What was there to say? Everything he said was true and there was nothing she could do to prove she hadn't been the one holding the knife when it sank over and over into the old man's chest.

"I'm going to read you your rights now," DuChien said before starting the memorized Miranda. She didn't really listen, too stunned to object when he cuffed her hands behind her back and helped her into the back of his police car. He reached across her to do the seatbelt, effectively locking her in place. This was really happening. She was getting arrested for a murder she didn't commit.

But in the back of her head she kept hearing a little voice reminding her she may not have killed Angus, but she'd killed Jonah. And by coming here she'd caused Angus' death. She leaned her head back against the worn vinyl seats, watching the sun rise.

Curious neighbors began to meander outside to see what the commotion was about. A lady in a bathrobe with a cigarette hanging from her lips held up her cell phone and snapped a picture.

A black sedan arrived on the scene and a woman exited the vehicle. She wore an all-black pants suit and when the cops went to shoo her away, she flashed them a badge of some kind and they waved her upstairs. Sloane barely paid attention focused on her own peril. This was bad. Really bad. To think yesterday she'd been worried about losing her license and now she was probably going to spend the rest of her life in jail.

She heard yelling and turned back to the bevy of officers surrounding the building. The front door of the museum slammed open, hitting the outside wall and swinging halfway back before it was caught by a slim, pink nailed hand.

"My supervisor will not be happy. This is definitely connected to the murder and theft at the warehouse outside of town. I need all of you searching for who did this. Knock on doors, canvas the neighborhood. Put this city's money to good use. There's a murderer on the loose and it's your job to find them."

Officer DuChien opened the door and slid in the driver's seat. "It shouldn't take long to get to the station, Miss Osborne. We'll get all this sorted out there."

While the engine revved, she turned back to see the woman step out of the museum door and her jaw dropped. It was Christa!

She was alive. Somehow, she'd gotten away from Xavier and his men! Maybe it meant Jonah was safe too. Maybe she'd saved them all. She knew how to use a gun, after all. Could Christa have fired those shots she'd heard when she was running away, not Xavier?

Two officers followed her out carrying Angus' body covered in a white cloth on a stretcher. As the car moved away, she turned back to face the front. She didn't usually pray but dipping her head toward her chin she did now, hoping desperately Angus had been reunited with Martha and was now at peace.

****

The police station was a madhouse. Drunk and disorderlies yelling obscenities through the bars at scantily dressed ladies brought in off the streets and men pacing because they did something stupid after losing their last dime. None of the glitter and sparkle of The Strip—here were the real stories. From the moment she stepped into the precinct, the whole place had the unsavory stench of stale coffee and cheap perfume.

A middle-aged detective escorted her into a sterile room with a dull tile floor containing a metal table with a chair on each side. He kept messing with what little hair he had left as if he could stop it receding by sheer will. As they entered, she saw him checking his reflection in the large mirror on one side of the room. She could tell it was a two-way glass mirror just like she'd seen on tv dramas and wondered who would be watching.

Where had Christa gone? She had so many questions for her, most of which she'd formulated on the short ride in the back of the police car. Like where was Jonah? Why had she left him? Was he ok? Why was she there? How had she found her so quickly? The list went on and on.

"Can I get you anything? Coffee? Water?" The officer asked before unlocking her wrists and gesturing to a chair.

"Water would be great," she replied, settling into the uncomfortable seat which made a loud creak when she slid it back so her shaking knees could be hidden by the table.

"I'll grab some for you. Someone will be in to talk with you shortly."

"Wait," she jumped up tailing him to the door. "Don't I get a phone call or something?"

"Only if it's necessary." He gave her a wry smile like he held all the cards and she held none. He pulled the door shut behind him.

What was probably twenty-minutes but felt like two hours later, the door finally opened, and she jerked to attention. Officer DuChien entered and set a cup of coffee in front of her on the table. It wasn't the water she'd asked for but at the moment her throat was so parched she didn't care. She took a sip and tried not to spit it back in the cup. It was absolutely the worst cup of coffee she'd ever tasted. Was that part of her punishment for what she'd done? Stale, gross coffee that tasted like crap in a cup?

Officer DuChien sat across from her, placing a small recording device, a manila file folder and a plastic bag with the word EVIDENCE in bold black letters on the table.

Sloane didn't need to look at the bag to know the sapphire knife was in the bag. As soon as he'd entered the room, she felt the stabbing sensation low in her back. The knife was still connected to her. It still wanted her blood.

DuChien wiped at his mustache with the back of his hand as if it tickled his nose before pressing record on the device as he opened the folder. "State your name and profession for the record."

That was an easy one. She could handle that.

"Sure, I mean…I'm Sloane Osborne. I'm a paranormal real estate agent."

He wrinkled his brow. "Say again?"

"I sell haunted houses."

He jotted something down and gave her his full attention, his expression not conveying a belief or disbelief in her profession.

"So you do believe the items in the museum were haunted, like you said."

"I do. I could feel the air growing heavy after he died."

"Then why were you in the museum?"

"I was calling you. The only phone he had was down there."

He made another note before rubbing at his mustache again. Sloane was suddenly seized by the urge to reach across the table and rip the stupid thing off his face.

"I see. What brings you to Las Vegas, Miss Osborne?"

Sloane leaned forward resting her elbow on the table and putting her forehead in her hand. This question was trickier.

She was stumped. Even after two hours of pondering how to proceed and knowing honesty was the best policy, who would believe her cockamamie story?

An FBI agent dragged her here for a secret assignment to help find a missing agent who was also Sloane's sometimes lover. She met a sicko with a private torture chamber who placed her in a room with two haunted knives. Stabbing her lover, she escaped the dungeon and fled to Angus Finch's home where he was stabbed in cold blood. Oh, and he had a scary doll whose head turned to follow when you walked around.

"I was asked to appear on a panel at a paranormal convention."

Extracting a flyer, he pointed to an agenda of the speakers at the conference. "Don't see you on here."

She scanned the names with him, with only the featured guest Jack Sackins' name jumping off the page at her. "I was a last-minute addition. As was Mr. Finch."

"Okay, so then what? How did you go from the

convention to Finch's? He was an old man so I'm not looking at a romantic angle and he didn't have any money to speak of, so you couldn't be looking for a handout. What reason would you have for being at his house in the middle of the night?" Closing the pamphlet and returning it to the file, he sat back and folded his arms over his chest.

"Well," she continued, "I got to talking with Mr. Finch while we sat together at the panel. I had a question about a possibly haunted object, and he suggested I come over today to discuss it with him."

"So you took a stolen van over to his place in only a jacket and a completely ripped dress covered in blood, which the forensic team is analyzing now. Then changed into some of his clothes and sat to have a heart to heart about a haunted object?"

Realizing now that this was not going well for her, she racked her brain to find the right way to explain her bizarre night. But there was nothing. There was no way she'd ever be able to make up a story believable enough to get her off. She might as well settle for the truth. It was the right thing to do anyway.

Right as she was opening her mouth to spill the whole tale, there was a brisk knock on the door and Christa strode into the interrogation room, head held high and boobs leading the way like directional lights. Flipping open a black wallet, she flashed her badge at Officer DuChien without a glance in Sloane's direction. Sloane didn't know how to play this. Was she supposed to act like she didn't know her? Would that help her case? Or should she admit she'd been working with Christa when all the bad stuff started happening.

"Thanks for starting the questioning, DuChien,"

Christa said, all business. "But this case has become FBI jurisdiction. The order from the central office is on your desk. This witness needs to be remanded into my care."

Stiffly, he stood up and gave her a curt nod. "I'll have to check on that."

Leaning down, he gathered his recording device and file folder, making sure the papers were neatly arranged inside. When he grabbed the evidence bag, Christa stopped him with a hand on his arm.

"You can leave that," she said.

DuChien looked at her, his eyes narrowing, as if he wasn't sure what to make of the comment.

"I have to file it with forensics for print identification," he said. "That should get Miss Osborne out of here faster. If you need the knife, it'll be in the evidence locker later."

Shaking off Christa's hand, he strode out the door without a backwards glance. She frowned, focusing her attention on Sloane only after the door had swung shut.

"Miss Osborne," Christa said, leaning both hands onto the table. "From what I hear, you've been the center of a lot of trouble since you got to Las Vegas."

"I…I…" she had no idea how to respond. She was more confused than when they'd been in Xavier's bathroom.

Christa leaned forward and whispered, "Don't worry. I'm going to get you out of here."

"How?" she asked, her voice just as low. She kept her hand around her awful cup of coffee for warmth in the air-conditioned room. "Jonah's dead and it's all my fault."

"It's not your fault. The FBI backup arrived too

late. It was just after you got out."

"Can I see his…him?" She couldn't bring herself to say his body.

"I'm sorry, Sloane. Arrangements are being made to get him home." There were tears in her eyes and she placed an arm around her.

She broke down, her legs buckling as her body failed her. She fell to her knees, heart-wrenching sobs tearing through her. It couldn't be true. He couldn't be gone. Gasping for breaths, she looked up at Christa, searching her face for the truth.

"I don't believe this," Sloane sobbed pointing a finger at her. "I would feel a void if he was gone, wouldn't I?"

It showed the amount of her shock and pain that she was asking Christa, who didn't believe in anything paranormal, these questions.

"I know you are in denial and angry right now and so am I. But because of you, Xavier's operation is shut down and he's in FBI custody. They're going to pin him for murder, abuse, kidnapping and probably a hundred more violations I can't think of right now. I just have to get that knife out of the evidence locker so I can use it to nail him for what he did to you and Jonah."

She dropped her arm from Sloane's shoulder, her face hardening into the mask Sloane recognized as an agent at work. She'd seen Jonah wear the expression often enough. "While I work on getting the knife transferred to the FBI. Pull yourself together, we still have a job to do. I already have someone working on the paperwork for your release. Hold tight and I'm sure someone will be here soon."

She wasn't listening. Before she could finish,

Christa was through the door, the scent of her floral perfume the only thing she left behind.

She could not compose herself before Officer DuChien returned.

"I've been given orders to release you," he said, tossing a file folder in front of her.

"What?" she asked, not believing Christa could really have managed to get her released so soon.

"It's against my better judgement but I don't have the authority to go against the FBI. A plane ticket has been purchased for you to Buffalo, New York. Agent McBride said a Stephanie Prescott will be waiting for you at the airport. You are to wait with her until you are contacted by an agent."

He rubbed at his mustache again, clearly agitated at being turned into a messenger.

"All right," she replied, taking several deep breaths. Christa had said something about getting Jonah home. That had to be why she was sending her to his Aunt Steph in Lily Dale, New York.

How would she ever be able to face Steph again? The woman would never forgive her. She'd never forgive herself.

But for the moment she needed to put one foot in front of the other. The first step was getting out of the police station. She had to pull herself together until she got to Lily Dale. Then she could break down.

"What do I need to do?"

"Just sign on the dotted line saying you understood the information I gave you. Then I have been instructed to drive you to your hotel to retrieve your things before taking you to the airport for your flight."

After signing the appropriate paperwork for her

release, she got a deep breath of fresh Vegas air. The sun was bright overhead. A single orb in a sea of blue without a cloud anywhere in sight. Officer DuChien helped her into the cruiser, without cuffing her this time, and she leaned back in the seat, letting the tears fall silently down her cheeks for the short trip to the hotel.

****

Her room at the X-cellence Hotel looked nothing like when she'd left it. All of Christa's bags were gone. All that was left was Sloane's black duffel bag with her own clothes and a pile of her personal items, including the handbag she'd had with her in Xavier's room with her ID and her phone. She had no idea how Christa had managed to get it back, but she was beginning to think it was better just to accept it and not ask questions. Especially since she had so many.

Plugging in her phone so it would charge, she took a quick shower, leaving the clothes Angus had given her in a neatly folded pile on the counter of the bathroom. It was nice to be back in something normal again, even if nothing about her life was ever going to be normal again. It wasn't fair. Most people went through life living with the one they loved. She didn't have that luxury. First, she'd lost Michael right before their wedding, now Jonah.

She wanted to cry but couldn't. It was as if her body was telling her she'd cried enough and there weren't any more tears to fall.

Shouldering her duffle, she grabbed her phone and headed down to where Officer DuChien waited to take her to the airport.

Chapter 11

The check-in line was at least fifty people deep when Officer DuChien left her at MacCarren International. Why couldn't the cheap FBI bastards have printed her boarding pass? *Seriously.* What a waste of time. She just wanted out of this city before anything else happened. Tapping her phone against her hip as she waited, she thought about calling Steph to make sure she'd really be at the airport to pick her up in Buffalo, but she knew she'd probably start crying again. There were too many people here for her to break down.

Besides, Christa had arranged everything so she was sure it would be fine. Speaking of Christa…she couldn't help but wonder what was going on? Would Jonah's body be on the same plane she was on or would he be taking a private flight? Probably private but she wanted to know for sure. She tried to text her: *What's going on? Where is Jonah?*

She waited, staring at the phone as she moved forward, one step closer to her boarding pass.

After at least twenty minutes and moving forward a few more times, there still wasn't an answer. Maybe Christa's phone had been lost last night.

To distract herself, Sloane opened the app for her equipment to see what'd been happening at the house in St. Louis. Watching the footage that triggered her motion detection sensors, she realized that the house in St. Louis was more active than ever, but the cameras showed her a different aspect of the boy than what she'd seen.

He wasn't violent or aggressive like he must have been to push Tori down the stairs. And he wasn't playful, like he'd been when she'd seen him. Instead, he spent his time wandering the rooms, sitting in a corner, or staring out the windows almost like he was waiting for someone. There wasn't a sign of the violent child she'd experienced in the house. Now the boy almost seemed…lonely.

Sloane felt a tug in her heart. If they tore down the house, it was possible the boy would be stuck there, unable to leave whatever was built in its place. A lot of times ghosts were tied to a location and not a physical building. If someone didn't help this boy move on, he could turn into something much worse than a prankster child but a truly horrible haunting, never able to move on.

It was like he was waiting for something. But what?

She needed to go back there at some point. She knew it. That boy needed her help.

But being in Buffalo with Aunt Stephanie was more important right now.

The phone buzzed in her hand and she glanced at the caller ID.

Taking a deep breath to calm the emotions bubbling to the surface and keep the tears at bay, Sloane answered.

"Hi, Steph. I…"

"Don't go to New York," Steph said abruptly,

cutting her off. "Meet me in St. Louis."

"What?"

"You have unfinished work there. I can sense it. And your career is on the line. We have to deal with that before anything else."

What was Steph talking about? She had been told to meet her in New York and though Officer DuChien hadn't said it, she'd gotten the impression she was being reprimanded into Steph's custody—as if there was still a chance she was in big trouble.

And then there was Jonah. Christa told her arrangements were being made to get him home. Steph was the only family she knew of, so wouldn't he be arriving there?

"But I can't. Jonah's going to be…"

"There's something else going on with him that neither of us are able to understand at the moment. I have this feeling everything will come together in St. Louis. We both need to be there. There's…"

"Steph, you have to listen to me. Jonah's dead."

"Did you see his dead body?"

"Well, no. I was there, and Christa said…."

"No, no. Sloane. FBI agents are not always agents of truth. Now, you will meet me in St. Louis, and we will get to the bottom of this."

Sloane knew more than to doubt Steph.

Going to St. Louis would still be meeting her at the airport and she'd still be with Steph, just like she was supposed to be. And she did feel like the boy in St. Louis needed her.

"All right, if that's all settled, there's a flight leaving in about twenty minutes," Steph cut into her thoughts. "I'm leaving now so we should get in around the same time, depending on weather. I'll meet you at the airport."

Steph didn't wait for a response, ending the call and leaving Sloane holding the phone to her ear, trying to sort her thoughts.

She really did feel like she needed to get to St. Louis. And if Steph thought everything, including what had happened to Jonah, would be resolved in Missouri, then that's where she needed to be.

"Next." She heard but didn't respond.

"Hey lady, it's your turn!" A man quipped.

Looking up, she realized he was talking to her and quickly stepping up to the counter where, the airline employee gave her quizzical look.

"Everything all right, Miss?"

"Yes, I'm fine. Could I get a ticket for your next flight to St. Louis? This is an emergency."

"If you're only carrying on, we have one leaving in twenty minutes," the lady replied, her fingers click-clacking on the keys as her eyes scanned the computer screen in front of her. "Otherwise we don't have another flight for eight hours."

"I'm not checking any bags," Sloane said, pulling out a credit card and handing it to the woman. "I'll take that flight."

"Gate seven," the woman said, printing out a boarding pass. "You'll need to hurry."

"Thanks, I will," she grabbed the piece of paper and hustled through the airport. There was a line at the metal detectors, but she somehow managed to squeeze in front of a family of seven and hustled up to the gate just as the doors were closing.

"Miss Osborne?" the gate attendant asked.

She nodded since she was hunched over, completely out of breath.

"I thought so. Got a call from Cindy at the front saying you were on your way. Come right aboard."

"Thanks."

She weaved her way through the already seated passengers to the lone empty seat at the back of the plane. She was shoved between a middle-aged man with his laptop already sitting on the fold down table and a young woman with a baby on her lap. She tossed her duffel into the overhead compartment before slumping into the seat and trying to catch her breath.

She closed her eyes, taking a deep breath and inhaling the smell of stale airplane air. The plane began to taxi toward the runway and the flight attendant started her spiel about securing her mask before helping someone else and how your seat cushion can be used as a floatation device.

She spent the first few minutes of the flight staring at the back of the seat in front of her and wondering what her life would be like without Jonah. It had almost killed her when Michael, her fiancé, had died. The only thing holding her to the world had been her belief she would see him again and her friendship with Jonah. But they'd moved beyond friends in the past year. She loved him. And now he was gone too. Or was he?

She bit down hard on the inside of her cheek to keep from crying. She'd been so sure she would know if he was gone. Something would be missing from inside her. They were connected in ways she didn't even try to understand. But she still felt the same. She couldn't understand it.

Finally, her brain gave out from lack of sleep and

she crashed for the rest of the three-hour flight, until the plane taxied to a stop at the terminal.

Arriving at the Lambert International Airport gave her a sense of Deja-vu. Only this time there wasn't a bitchy real-estate agent waiting for her with a car. Instead it was Aunt Steph, looking the same as the first time she'd met her.

She was thin as a stick wearing a black billowy peasant-style dress and layers of silver jewelry that made her look like some sort of gothic gypsy. Her hair was streaked with a deep red this time, not the purple she remembered from Maine, but her face was still the same and her eyes were just like Jonah's.

"There's my girl," Steph said with a small smile, opening her arms.

As Steph wrapped her thin arms around her shoulders, she finally allowed herself to cry. She sobbed, her tears soaking into Steph's dress as the woman stroked her hair and mumbled words she couldn't understand.

She cried not only for Jonah, but for Angus and for herself too. Everything would be different now. She would be different now and it was nice to be hugged by someone who cared about her and loved Jonah too.

"Feel better now?" Steph asked, as Sloane hiccupped herself dry.

She stepped back, rubbing her eyes, a little embarrassed by her display.

"No, sorry."

"Nothing to apologize for. You were hurt and you needed to let those feelings out. But, if you're ready, we need to take that first step forward toward healing."

"Have you heard anything about Jonah's body?"

"I haven't," Steph replied, her eyes narrowing in thought. "Which I find a little odd. I've reached out to my contacts at the FBI and no one has any information for me. For all I know he could be so deep undercover, they can't tell me about it, he could be dead, or he could be in a really bad mood and not want to talk to me."

"Stop believing everything you can hear. I've been trying to tell you that. But right now, while we wait, the best thing we can do to occupy our minds is work. I've seen the little boy and the outside of this house in my dreams for weeks. That's why I'm here. What do you think we need to do?"

So like Steph to get right down to business.

"That's the thing, I have no idea where to start."

"I find it's good to start at the beginning, of course. There's a reason we're in St. Louis. Why don't you explain that to me first?"

Sloane quickly explained the call she'd gotten from Tori Jensen and the young boy haunting the house. She didn't leave anything out, including Carolyn's blackmail attempt and what she'd seen on her equipment. As she spoke she felt the boy's loneliness again. He needed to move on, and she knew she was supposed to help him.

Steph listened, still resting one hand on her shoulder in a comforting gesture though she knew the woman was probably using the connection to learn more about the situation from her feelings.

"I see," Steph said when she was done, her eyes narrowing in thought. "This does seem to be a problem. What do *you* think you should do?"

For a moment she didn't know what to say. Usually Steph told her what to do and expected her advice to be followed to the letter. She didn't remember her ever once asking for her opinion. But after a brief hesitation, she realized she did have the beginnings of a plan.

The boy was waiting for someone. She needed to find *Sissy*.

Suddenly Sloane understood and felt like an idiot for not seeing it sooner. It wasn't Sissy he was asking for, but his *sister*.

"I think the owner, the old woman who is selling the house, needs to come back. I think she's the only one who can release the boy."

Steph's smile said her instincts in the situation were spot on.

"Then get on the phone with that agent and let's find out where she is."

****

Steph had rented a tiny red hatchback so different from the huge Buick she drove in New York it was laughable. The car was half the size and twice as fast, something Sloane found out firsthand as Steph drove the ten miles to the house. Sloane called Tori, explaining the situation and Tori had promised to try her best to get Mildred, the owner, back to the house. The woman's health had taken a turn and Tori wasn't sure the hospital would release her, but she'd see what she could do.

She barely recognized the block when she rounded the corner and parked in front of the house. Most of the neighborhood was surrounded by the temporary fences used by construction companies with yellow caution tape warning people away. A bunch of trucks; a loader, excavator and even a bulldozer, were on the corner lot, where one of the neighboring houses had recently been demolished. Mounds of dark gray cement and rubble filled the empty place where the house used to be. The beautiful neighborhood looked more like a warzone than a city block.

She was confused. From what Carolyn had said, the whole neighborhood had to sell for the plans for the hotel to go through. There had to be more holdouts than just Mildred, didn't there? There'd been those two sisters she'd met out front. Had they been forced to sell too? Or had Carolyn somehow managed to get the work pushed through without everyone's capitulation?

Using the code, Sloane opened the door, taking a deep breath before stepping inside. She didn't want to admit why she was nervous. Michael had been a year and a day kind of guy, always saying they'd do things; go on a cruise, try a new restaurant, or even get married in a year and a day. She'd made contact with him exactly a year and a day after he'd died. Jonah was different.

If he was dead, he wouldn't wait. She didn't want to open the door and see him checking her equipment and giving his personal opinion on the haunting.

But when she pushed open the door, the house was empty. She didn't feel Jonah's presence at all. Wandering room to room, she checked her equipment for any new activity. There wasn't much. The only time the boy seemed to overreact was the onetime Carolyn had visited, all alone.

Sloane wanted to applaud when she saw the video showing the little boy making every picture in the house fly at the real-estate agent's head as she walked past.

"Hello?" Sloane said, loudly, hoping her voice carried through the house. "It's me again. I've come back to help you."

"Sissy?" a small voice asked behind her.

"No, dear, I'm not Sissy," Sloane said. "But I have a feeling she will be here soon."

She'd seen the picture on the wall of the young girl and boy when she'd come with Carolyn. Something about it had touched her. Now she thought she knew why.

"Aren't you going to introduce us?" Steph asked as if they were at a social gathering not meeting with a ghost.

"I'm sorry," Sloane replied. "Aunt Steph, this is... You know what, I don't actually know your name."

"His name is Phillip," a raspy voice said behind her.

Sloane turned to see a frail old lady being carried up the stairs by a tall man in pale blue scrubs. Behind him, a young woman in a pantsuit and a female nurse dressed in scrubs patterned with pineapples on them lifted a wheelchair up the handful of steps and into the front entry.

When the wheelchair was set, the man placed the old lady in it, her slight frame barely took up half of the wide seat. She crossed her stick-like legs at the ankles as the nurse covered her with a dark blue lap blanket. Her hands shook when she reached for the corners of her worn gray cardigan and closed the front. Wispy strands of kinky white hair clung to her head but did nothing to hide the age spotted skin on her scalp. Her face was wrinkles upon wrinkles, but she smiled at Sloane, her green eyes showing her mind was still sharp, even if her body was failing her.

"You must be Mildred, the owner," Sloane said, stepping forward to gently shake the old woman's hand.

"I am," she replied. "And this is Tori, the one you spoke to on the phone,"

"Hello, Tori. It's nice to finally meet you." Sloane shook her hand as well. "Thank you for arranging for Mildred to be here. To be honest, I wasn't sure we'd be able to pull this off. When I called, you sounded doubtful you'd be able to get Mildred from the hospital."

"I didn't think I'd be able to," Tori replied. "But when I mentioned I had a paranormal expert waiting for her at the house, Mildred tried to pull out her own IV. There was no saying no to her."

"She threatened to call both her lawyer and a cab if we didn't let her out," the male nurse said with a laugh. "Delores and I were the compromise."

"Well, thank you all for coming. This is Steph, another paranormal expert and she will be helping me today while we try to help…Phillip, did you say? He was your brother, right?"

She turned back to Mildred. The old woman wasn't looking at her but staring toward the spot where the small boy stood. Her eyes shifted to the right and left though, as if searching for something she knew was there but couldn't see. With a sad smile, the boy disappeared.

"Yes, Phillip," she whispered. "He was my baby brother.

"He was the only sibling I had who lived past a day or two. I remember whenever it stormed, he'd find his way into my bed and I'd snuggle him close and tell him stories about a thunder king who lived in the sky and battled demons away with fists like hammers, creating the thunder and lightning whenever he wholloped a creature trying to make their way to earth. It was silly but it used to make him smile.

"Our father was hard on him. Demanding, really. Wanted him to act like a man when he was only ever a boy. That's how he died too. Father sent him on an errand, and he walked in front of a buggy. If only I'd gone with him that day."

"I'm sure it wasn't your fault," Sloane told her. "And he didn't blame you. There would be an aura of anger hanging over the house if he did. I only sense a mischievous boy. You sense him too, but you can't see him, can you?"

"I've known he was here since the day he died," Mildred replied. "I remember they laid him out in his nicest suit in front of the fireplace. I could see him lying there looking so still and quiet, but it was always like he was at the edge of my vision. If I'd turned a second faster, I could have spotted him or if I'd listened harder, I would hear his voice."

"How old were you when he died?" Steph asked.

"I'd just turned fifteen and Phillip was almost five. We've been together ever since," she reached out to Sloane, taking her hand in a placating gesture. "I didn't know what to do when I got too sick to live here. I was afraid whoever bought the house would do something to him—like chase him out of the only home he's ever known. They wouldn't understand him like I do. He's just a boy, after all. That's why I didn't want to sell to that horrible woman. I needed someone compassionate to buy the house."

"It's all right," Sloane told her. "I understand but I think we're at the point where keeping the house from being torn down is almost impossible. What we need to do is work together to figure out how to help Phillip move on."

"How do we do that?" Mildred asked, clasping her boney hands in her lap so tight they reddened while her knuckles turned a bright yellowy-white.

"I'm not positive." She glanced at Steph, expecting her to step in with her opinion but she tipped her head to the side, her expression definitely telling her this was her mess and she needed to solve it. "But I suspect there's a reason he never moved on. With most ghosts there's some unfinished business or something they regret holding them here. Until they've gotten some conclusion or made up for past mistakes, their guilt keeps them trapped. Can you think of anything like that with Phillip?"

"A regret? Unfinished business? Besides dying when he was just a child?" Mildred asked, her brow creased with confusion. "He was such a sweet and loving boy, even after our Mama died and he had to put up with me raising him instead. I always knew I was a better sister than a mother, probably why I never had any children myself."

She sighed heavily, closing her eyes. Her lids were pale blue and almost transparent. As she exhaled, her shoulders slumped, and it looked like her whole body was folding in on itself.

"If you don't mind me asking, what's wrong with you?" Steph asked quietly, stepping forward. She knelt down so her face was level with Mildred's laying a hand on the old woman's arm. "I sense pain in you. It's only your sheer will that's keeping you here."

"I'm old," Mildred replied. "Just two months shy of ninety-nine. This body wasn't made for that many years. The number of tubes and monitors they had on me in the hospital, it was hard to remember why I needed to hold on. But I had to…"

"What did you have to do?" Sloane asked, kneeling on the other side of the wheelchair.

"I had to make sure he'd be ok," Mildred said, opening her eyes. She looked at Sloane with such intensity, Sloane could feel the pain and longing inside the green gaze.

"Are you his anchor?" she asked softly. "Do you think he could be waiting for you?"

"Sissy?"

Mildred's head snapped up, focusing on where Phillip stood on the bottom step of the spiraling staircase. She reached out blindly, grabbing Sloane's hand on one side and Steph's on the other in a tight grip. Her hands were so cold it was as if she was balancing on a thin line between the living and the dead.

The two nurses moved forward, as if to help, but Sloane waved them back with her free hand. Reluctantly, Delores went to stand by Tori, but the male nurse grabbed the back of the wheelchair. At first Sloane thought he didn't trust them, then she noticed his eyes were focused on the boy at the bottom of the stairs, too.

"Is it finally time, then?" Phillip asked. *"Are you ready to go? I've been waiting an awfully long time."*

"I see him. Is he really there? Is that my Phillip?"

Mildred glanced at Steph, who Sloane noticed had

tears in her eyes.

"It's all right," Steph said. "It's him."

"Are you sure?' Mildred asked, turning to Sloane. "And he'll be ok if I just let go?"

"I think you both will," Sloane told her. "Sometimes the bond of love transcends all things. His love for you kept him here until you were ready. He's waited, watching over you and keeping you safe, as you did when he was alive. I think it's time for the two of you to be together again."

"Come on, Sissy. It's time to go."

He reached out a hand to her and Mildred took it. As she stood, her spirit separated from her body. The body in the wheelchair slumped into the seat as her spirit continued to step tentatively forward. She glanced back over her shoulder, a sweet smile on her face as Phillip led her up the stairs.

When they reached the top, a blinding light flashed so bright Sloane had to look away, when she turned back the two spirits were gone.

"You did good, kid," Steph said, reaching over to close Mildred's staring eyes.

"Thanks," Sloane replied, though she didn't feel like she'd done anything good. One success in her professional work didn't get rid of the pain in her heart. "Can you help gather my equipment? There's one more thing left to do, and then we can get out of here."

One of the nurses double-checked Mildred for a pulse but after shaking his head, Delores went outside and returned with a clean, white sheet, draping it over Mildred's small form with tears in her eyes.

"I've never seen anything like that. Have you Scott?" Delores said as the man shook his head. "It was

159

like she really went to the light. In all my years…"

"Do we need to call the morgue," Tori asked.

"I'll take care of it," Delores said, as Scott picked up Mildred's body to carry outside.

While Steph gathered Sloane's paranormal equipment, she signed the paperwork Carolyn had left on the counter in the kitchen. Sliding the pile of paperclipped papers to the back of the counter, she listened to the sounds of the house. Everything, from the nurses' voices to Tori's shoes in the hall echoed through the walls. The place felt empty now. Just as it was needed to be.

Pulling out her cell, she texted Carolyn.

It's done. The paperwork is on the counter. And keep your money. I don't want or need it. I hope you're happy now.

The reply came almost immediately.

So glad you saw reason. Here's a copy of your reinstated license. I pulled a few strings to get it for you. And yes, I am happy.

Sloane wanted to punch someone. Preferably Carolyn but she'd take just about anyone right now. Xavier. One of his guards. Even Jonah. Oh, she'd love to punch Jonah because that would mean he was alive. She hated when evil people got their way. Carolyn was like the perfect mean girl at school who treated everyone like crap but, for some unexplained reason, all the teachers loved.

Even though clearing the house had been the right thing to do, she felt a hollow pit in the center of her chest knowing that Carolyn had won, and she'd lost everything, all in one weekend.

"I think that's everything," Steph said, coming into

the kitchen. "Unless you've purchased some new equipment since the last time I saw you."

"No, can't afford that," she half smiled.

"I meant what I said, by the way. You did good. I know you've had a rough time of it and waiting for word on Jonah is eating at you, but you still managed to do what needed to be done. You've grown since Maine."

"That means a lot."

"I can sense by your aura you don't believe me. You're not your usual tangerine today. More of a brownish green mess going on which means you're worried. Why don't we find a hotel room and you can lay down?"

"I have a hotel room, but I don't feel like taking a nap right now. It's a great room. Why don't you go. I saw a wine bar around the corner. I think I'll stop there for a drink, or seven."

"Are you sure that's what you need?" Steph asked. She'd always had a thing about drinking. Something about it interfering with the ability to ward off evil spirits.

Right now, she didn't care.

"Sometimes what you want and what you need are two very different things," she replied. "And at the moment I want a drink."

Chapter 12

The wine bar was on Cherokee Street and had a name she couldn't pronounce but advertised a delicious watermelon rum slushy that sounded to die for. Pushing the heavy door open, she heard a bell ting as she entered.

"Good afternoon," a woman threw over her shoulder, scampering after an escaped toddler with a shock of blonde hair. "It'll be just a minute."

She corralled the little girl in a corner before lifting her off her feet and laughing as she tossed her in the air. Sloane took a seat at the end of the bar closest to the door. The other end was already occupied, though the man wasn't really there. He sat loose and relaxed in his three-piece suit, suspenders, and spectacles watching the child, she had a feeling the woman had no idea he was there.

"All right, the mommy monster has to work now. You sit here and be good." She plopped the child down in a corner booth with crayons scattered across the table and a few dolls sitting in the seat like paying customers.

"Sorry about that," the woman said, brushing her shoulder-length brown hair out of her eyes. "My sister went for supplies. When she gets back one of us can cart her to our apartment upstairs."

"You're the owner then? It's a nice place." Sloane said, admiring the décor. The place had an Italian feel with brown woodwork and lots of windows.

"I am. My sister and I own the place. My name's Beckie but haven't we met before?"

"I don't think so. I'm just visiting…"

Beckie interrupted her by snapping her fingers so loudly Sloane jumped.

"I remember now. It was a couple days ago. Outside Mildred's place. It was the morning Katie—that's my twin—made a big deal about getting up and taking a walk. You were with Carolyn Miller."

Sloane nodded, vaguely remembering the meeting.

"I was investigating something at the house," Sloane told her. "I don't usually associate with people like Carolyn Miller."

Beckie laughed so loud her daughter looked over to see what was happening.

"No, I wouldn't expect anyone would want to associate with her. Is Mildred still holding out like us?"

"I'm sorry to tell you Mildred passed away. I doubt there will be a way to keep Carolyn from buying the place now."

"That's too bad," Beckie frowned. "This place has been in our family for years. I really don't want to sell but unless we come up with a bundle of cash… But what am I bothering you about that for. What can I get you?"

"Can I have one of those?" Sloane asked, gesturing to the slushy machine.

"Here I am talking about my problems when I can see you seem like you're having a rough day," Beckie said, filling Sloane a glass of the chilly pink mixture.

"What would make you say that?" She didn't look at the woman when she answered.

"I've been behind this bar practically my whole life," Sloane caught the man at the end of the bar smile sadly at Beckie's words. "I know when someone's having a rough time of it. My great uncle would roll over in his grave if I couldn't spot someone who needed a drink and a listening ear. And he'd probably come back and wallop me himself if he knew I hadn't offered it. So, spill. Tell me all about it." The woman leaned over the bar, resting her chin on her hand, her eyes not really questioning, just wondering.

"I'm not sure I'm ready to talk," Sloane admitted, swirling the straw in her slushy. "I might need a few more of these first."

The woman's eyes narrowed, and she stood, stretching her arms over her head.

"You know what goes with slushies? Pizza. You want some pizza? It's on the house. At least, as long as you like chocolate pizza because that's what she likes," she nodded toward her tow-headed daughter who had set up what might have been a tea party with her dolls at the bar.

"Chocolate pizza?"

"It's a house specialty. It's called The Tillie after my niece. All the kids love it."

"That sounds delicious?" Sloane wasn't sure she wanted to try it but didn't want to offend the woman and her house specialty.

"Oh, God no. It's terrible. Only the kids like it. I'd never force an adult to eat the thing!" she laughed. "I'll make you my favorite instead. That bundle of energy, by the way, is Cher."

"I'm Sloane," she replied.

Beckie disappeared through a small door behind

the bar which Sloane guessed led to the kitchen. Almost immediately a stringy haired doll with pen marks on her once beautiful face appeared on the bar next to Sloane's drink.

"Hi," Sloane said. To the girl, not the doll.

"That's Greta," the child whispered. "She's a good listener."

Great. Now children were trying to cheer her up.

"Really? Do you tell her all your stories?" Sloane asked.

"Uh-huh," Cher nodded. "And she never talks back like he does."

The girl pointed to the old man at the end of the bar.

Sloane wasn't surprised the girl could see the ghost. Children were often more sensitive than adults.

"Does he like to tell you stories too?" Sloane asked.

"He likes to talk about his money," Cher continued.

He looked up, his sad eyes meeting Sloane's and he smiled a little. Sloane looked back down at her drink.

The girl climbed down from the bar stool, heading toward her coloring book in the corner. Her timing was perfect because at that moment Beckie returned through the swinging kitchen door, wiping her hands on her apron.

"Two pizzas in the oven. Just be a few minutes until they're done. The best thing about owning this bar is the pizza. I love pizza. Well, I love alcohol too, but that's beside the point."

Sloane actually managed to laugh.

"See, I am funny," Beckie said. "I knew it. My twin, Katie, always says she's the funny one but she's obviously wrong. I've also been told I'm good at listening without judging. It's part of the job."

"Without judging, huh?" Sloane asked.

"None whatsoever. Whatever you've done, I've most likely attempted worse. I went to a Catholic High School. You know how Catholic girls are."

"Pious?"

"Hell no! Rebellious! Now come on. Tell me what's bothering you."

The front door jingled the bell hanging over it when it was pushed open, admitting a woman who could only have been Beckie's twin carrying a heavy looking grocery bag in one arm.

"Speak of the devil," Beckie said with a laugh.

"Devil? No, I've been trying to tell you since we were kids, I'm the good one." She placed a hand over her chest as if honestly hurt by her sister's statement.

Even in the mood she was in, Sloane managed a soft chuckle.

"Hey, Katie, come on over here. This is my new friend Sloane. She hates Carolyn Miller too."

Katie carried her brown bag of groceries to the bar, handing them over the counter to her sister.

"Katie, Sloane. Sloane, Katie," Beckie said as if that constituted an introduction. "Sloane was about to tell me what's bothering her so I can help."

"Good. After we help her maybe we can tell her about our problems, and she can help us."

"What's your problem?" Sloane asked, her interest piqued. It was easier to help others than herself.

"Nothing," Beckie replied immediately. A timer

dinged in the back and she grabbed the bag of groceries before heading through the small door to the kitchen.

"Nothing?" Katie called after her. "You call losing this bar nothing? Because that's what's going to happen if we don't come up with about a hundred thousand dollars in the next two days."

"What are you talking about? Why are you losing the bar? I thought you said it had been in the family for years?" Sloane asked.

"It has been. But we needed money to fix things up, so we remortgaged it a few years ago. Worst decision we ever made. The bank called in our loan because a developer is buying all the land around here and paying top dollar for everything so he can build his big casino. From the plans I've seen, this wonderful establishment," she flung her arms out, gesturing to the bar around them "is set to become a parking lot. We have two days to pay our loan in full before they close our bar, tear it down, and pave it over. We're the last holdout on this block. Everyone else sold long ago. Probably should have given in then."

"What happens if you come up with the money?" Sloane asked.

"Then we ruin everyone's plan and I get to have the best day ever," Katie replied, blowing her bangs out of her eyes with a puff of air as she sat on the stool next to Sloane, reaching over the bar to pour herself a drink. "Not that it's going to happen."

"Wouldn't that be great though," Sloane mused, finishing off her slushie. Without even asking, Katie refilled her glass. "I'd love to see the look on her face if she didn't get what she wanted."

"What did she do to you?" Katie leaned on the bar,

her attention focused.

"I'm a real-estate agent and I was called in to deal with a problem with a house. When I got here Carolyn met me at the airport and threatened to ruin my career if I didn't do what she said so the sale can go through."

"What a raging B…."

"Pizza's ready!"

Beckie returned with a small pizza topped with chocolate and bananas and a larger with cheese, ham, and pineapple, sliding them onto the bar.

"Dig in," she said, handing Sloane a plate before taking the chocolate pizza over to her daughter's table and serving her a piece. "Katie, can I talk to you in the kitchen, please?"

"What is it now?" Katie asked, reaching for a slice of pie.

"It's about the groceries you got."

"If she'd wanted anything special, she should have given me a list," Katie grumbled, dropping the pizza and slouching after her sister and leaving Sloane alone with the toddler and the ghostly old man again.

She pulled off a slice, placing it in front of her, but didn't start eating. There was too much to think about. She knew she should eat but she just wasn't hungry. Even though she'd succeeded in helping Mildred and Phillip move on, she was still sad the house would get torn down. It was such a beautiful place and was going to be completely gone, without a trace.

And this place. To think these two girls, who seemed like genuinely good people, were going to lose not only their home in the apartment upstairs, but also their business. They'd lose everything in one fell swoop.

If only there was a way to stop all this. If only there was some money lying around.

A spark of an idea surfaced.

"Excuse me, sir," she said, turning to the man still seated at the end of the bar. "Do you know these girls?"

"These girls are my great-nieces." He didn't seem surprised she could see him. "Their father was named after me."

"And are you here to help them? Is that your unfinished business?" Sloane asked.

"I've been sitting here so long waiting for someone to notice me, I'm not sure what my business is anymore," the old man smiled, running a hand over the wispy hairs on top of his head. "And now it's too late to help them."

"Tell her about the stuff under the stairs," Cher said, peering around the man at Sloane, chocolate smeared all over her cheeks. "Maybe she can find it for you."

"What's under the stairs?" Sloane asked.

"Exactly what they need!" The man stood, his eyes lighting with hope. "I got them from my grandpappy and he from his, but I didn't have any kids of my own to pass it on to. I hid it in the secret compartment behind the cabinet to keep it safe. I was going to write to them about it, but I died before I could tell them."

"I'll check it out," she said, pulling herself to her feet. "If you help me."

Holding out her hand, Cher led the way past the bathroom to the back of the bar and down a creepy staircase to the basement. At the bottom of the stairs, they turned to see in large wooden cabinet built to fit perfectly in the empty triangular area beneath the steps.

She and Cher opened the cabinet door, pushing things aside and taking out the things blocking the back.

"Hey! What are you two doing down here?" Beckie demanded, appearing behind them so suddenly it made Sloane jump. Katie was right behind her, hands on her hips and heated anger in her eyes.

"We've been trying to help you, and this is how you repay us?" Katie demanded.

"I know it sounds crazy, but Cher and I just had a chat with your great-uncle. Could you get me a prybar or a hammer or something?"

Katie reached around her back and pulled out some pepper spray, aiming it at Sloane's face. "Cher, get over here right now."

To the little girl's credit, she stood her ground and squeezed Sloane's hand. "They never believe me. I tell them he sits there but they can't see him, so they think I'm making it up." She turned to her mom and aunt, mimicking her aunt's hands on hips stance. "You better listen to this lady or else!"

Sloane felt the tension mounting. She inherently knew that she was an oddball. Saw ghosts. Received messages. Asked people to take crazy leaps of faith. But here she was in someone's establishment, with one of their children, asking for a crowbar. She'd sunk to a new level of crazy.

"Look, I'm really sorry. Let's start again. I'm Sloane Osborne, I'm a paranormal investigator and real-estate agent. I sell haunted houses. Maybe you've heard of me?" Beckie crossed her arms over her chest, completely blocking the stairway.

Sloane took that as a no.

"Anyway, I was really brought to St. Louis to help

clear Mildred's house. It'd been haunted by the ghost of her younger brother. I helped both him and Mildred move on. Then I'm sitting at your bar and there's an old man there saying something about money."

Katie lowered the pepper spray. "I should have recognized you. I remember you from the tv! Didn't that guy in Wisconsin almost kill you? But you got out and exposed a huge serial killer."

"Yes, that's me but it wasn't like that." Just thinking about it made her crave a glass of water.

"You really saw our Great Uncle?" Katie asked.

"Old guy, bald, wears his pants really high with suspenders."

"That's him," Beckie said, throwing her hands up in the air and giving up the fight. "And I can see I'm in the minority here since I still think you're crazy. I'll see if I can find a hammer before Katie destroys the basement looking for one."

After knocking on several spots in the back of the wooden cabinet, she found the hollow sounding area and was able to pry off the slats covering the secret compartment. Reaching into a cobweb-filled hole that went into the stone wall behind the piece of furniture, she pulled out a dusty wooden box about the size of a loaf of bread but much heavier.

"What in the world?" Katie said when Sloane handed her the box. "Was he hiding this from us?"

"Like I told you, I saw your uncle upstairs. He's somehow tied to the bar. He told me he was about to write you two a letter before he died. He wanted you to know this was here in case you needed it, but he ran out of time. Whatever is in that box, it's for the two of you."

Beckie and Katie sat cross-legged on the floor and examined the box. It said, *Sutter's Fort Store Coloma, California.* Using the back end of the hammer they pried off the lid and pushed aside the wood shavings. Inside little packets of cheesecloth were golden nuggets about the size of pebbles, some the size of irregular-shaped golf balls.

The girls sifted the rocks through their fingers. "Holy shit, Katie. Remember the stories Big Uncle Bob used to tell about our great-great-great-great-grandad and the gold rush. This is it! This must be the treasure he found! We're going to be able to keep the bar!"

"Take that Carolyn Miller!" Katie pumped a fist in the air in triumph.

Sloane smiled. It was great to know Carolyn was going down. That lady really was a fabulous bitch. Her only wish was she could be there when the woman found out. She'd love to hear her scream. She might even break down and cry.

Putting her vengeance behind her, she headed to the stairs and saw the old man standing at the top. He gave a solemn nod before a light seemed to engulf him and he disappeared.

Trying to be unobtrusive, she left them to their treasure and headed back to the pizza she'd left behind.

Sitting at the bar, she picked up a slice as the bell over the door announced someone's entry. In the quiet, she heard the bolt of the lock slip into place. Cocking her head in confusion, Sloane started to turn, when a familiar voice spoke behind her.

"Hey, Sloane. Miss me?"

"Christa! What are you doing here?" Sloane asked, jumping to her feet and turning around. "I thought you were still in Las Vegas. Do you have any news about Jonah?"

Even though a few days ago she'd hated this woman, Sloane couldn't have been happier to see her. Not only had they sort of bonded over make-overs and kidnappings, but she was Sloane's only connection with Jonah. She hoped deep within her soul the woman had traveled to the Gateway City with good news.

But the look on her face said otherwise. Her blue eyes blazed with fire and, for the first time in Sloane's memory, the blonde bombshell did not look perfect. Her hair was pulled back in a bun at the nape of her neck, but her part was crooked, and wisps of hair stuck out like porcupine quills. Her black suit was wrinkled and there was a brown stain on her light pink shirt that looked like blood.

"Where is it?" Christa demanded.

"Where is what?" Sloane asked.

"Don't be coy with me, you slutty little bitch. You know where it is."

Sloane glanced around the bar as if the windows and walls might give her a clue what Christa was talking about, but she really didn't have any idea.

Christa's heels click-clacked on the hardwood floor as she approached the bar. Sloane backed up until her back hit the counter, a bar stool on either side, caging her between the bar and Christa.

"What?"

Christa raised an arm and she cringed, expecting a blow but instead the blade of the ruby-encrusted knife slammed into the countertop next to her, the hilt swaying from the force, the rubies glinting in the light.

Sloane recoiled, her eyes on the blade. She knew

that knife. Knew the rubies and gold in the hilt and the wavy silver edge. The last time she'd seen it, the blade had been protruding from Jonah's chest.

"I'll be needing the other knife, Sloane," Christa snarled, her breath tickling Sloane's ear. "Did you think you could get away with stealing it from the evidence room. I know someone was working with you on this. Was it that policeman? Officer DuChien? Is he the one who took it for you?"

"I don't know what you're talking about," she replied, pushing her hands out in a placating gesture, trying to calm Christa down. "I never worked with anyone but you. I didn't even know Officer DuChien until he arrested me. And I never want to see those knives again. That knife killed Jonah."

From the corner of her eye she saw the child, Cher, crouching beside the bar. The little girl's eyes were wide, her face pale. Sloane half smiled at her, lifting her chin to point toward the back stairs where her mom and aunt were still examining their treasure. She wanted to scream to the girl to run but didn't want to draw Christa's attention to the child.

"Don't lie to me anymore. You were the only one besides me who knew Officer DuChien was putting the knife in the evidence locker. Then you waylaid me with your crying and sobbing so when I got there it was gone. If only the damn thing hadn't gotten stuck in the old man's chest."

"Old man's...? Are you talking about Angus? How do you know that? They'd already moved him when you got there."

Christa's eyes glittered and Sloane suddenly saw her in a completely different way than she ever had before. Gone was the ditzy blonde bimbo who was Jonah's partner and the smart, vivacious woman she'd worked with in Vegas. Instead she saw a cold-blooded killer.

"Do you know what these knives are worth?" Christa demanded. "But you have to have the set. No one wants one of them. They have to have both. I know you have the knife so where is it?" Christa grabbed the back of Sloane's head with one hand, her long fingernails digging into her scalp.

Sloane's mind was buzzing as another piece fit into the puzzle. "You killed Angus?"

This was all a set-up? Christa got her to Vegas to get near the knives? It was all her fault. All of it.

"You weren't supposed to get out of Xavier's facility. Jonah should have killed you when he had the chance. But instead he was heroic and tried to save you. Look where that got him."

Christa was so flippant talking about her partner, as if Jonah hadn't mattered to her at all. But in a way, Sloane felt her words ring true. He'd sacrificed himself to save her. She wished Jonah had been able to kill her instead. He hadn't deserved any of this. She did.

"So I was just part of the show?" she guessed. "You needed me so the two knives would react, and Xavier would get his murder footage. Are you working for him now, too?"

"You have no idea what you're talking about. I just need the knife. Let's say, for the FBI. But I don't really care what you think anymore. Give it to me and this will all be over. If you hadn't taken the knife in the first place I wouldn't have had to go after you and that idiot museum director wouldn't have had to die. But you did.

His blood is on your hands. Now, tell me where you hid the knife."

"Sloane?" Beckie tentatively said her name from the stairway. Sloane leaned back to look at the woman, as Christa wrenched the ruby hilted knife from the counter.

"Oh great, more witnesses," Christa complained, losing her normally cool and collected focus on the task at hand. She was—as the kids say—*triggered.*

"Take your sister and Cher and get out of here. No matter what, don't come back today," she tried to keep her voice calm and steady though it did crack on the little girl's name. Christa was an unhinged murderer. She'd killed Finch. And set up Jonah to get captured. Who knew what she'd do to these innocent bystanders?

There was a brief moment of hesitation and she thought the bartender might try to help her out, but protecting her daughter won, and the three of them raced out the back door.

"All right, now that we're alone do you feel more like talking?" Christa asked slowly walking after the twins and locking the door. "We have about three minutes before the cops show up and I have to shoot you. Tell me now or die. Your choice."

Sloane slowly turned to really look at Christa. She was nothing like the woman who'd barged into her bathroom and demanded she get out of the bathtub. In fact, she looked like she hadn't slept since Vegas. She looked deranged but Sloane realized she felt the same way. This woman had been the cause of her life falling to pieces. She wasn't going to cooperate. Fuck Christa and whatever her endgame was.

"I don't know where your precious knife is," she

repeated. "The last time I saw it was in the interrogation room at the police station. You were there."

"But I searched the evidence locker. I looked everywhere. I tore that disgusting place apart. The knife wasn't there. I even drilled DuChien and he wouldn't break." Christa twirled the knife between her fingers without looking at it, as if playing with a knife was a common, habitual action for her. "If you don't have it, you must have been working with someone. Who was helping you?"

Sloane shrugged, not knowing what to tell her.

"You don't understand," Christa pointed the knife at Sloane's chest, stepping forward. Her eyes were wide, her pupils dilated with fear and anger. "I need that knife. I have to have the matched set."

"Why do you need the knives?" Sloane asked.

"As if I'd tell you," Christa sneered. "Bringing you to Vegas was supposed to be my 'in' with all those crazies at the convention but you ruined everything, just like usual."

"You know the cops are probably on their way," Sloane told her, hoping it would make a difference, but doubting it all the same.

"Good," Christa replied with a smirk on her red lips. "I'm here to arrest a murderer. I'm FBI, remember? They will listen to me."

Something clicked inside her head as if the puzzle was finally fitting together. She felt so dumb for not seeing it sooner.

"No, they won't. You've gone rogue, haven't you?"

Christa's expression became guarded, as if she realized she'd finally said too much.

"None of this is FBI sanctioned. This has always been about you and what you wanted. To think I was actually starting to think you weren't half bad but then your true colors shine through and they're showing ugliness indeed. Did Jonah know?"

"Jonah didn't need to know. Do you know what it's like at the FBI? All the grueling training just to go out there and put your life on the line for people you don't even know. And for what? A lousy pittance of a salary and thankless people who demand everything. Sometimes I even I hate the idea of sharing the same air with them, let alone going out of my way to help."

Yeah, it's called service to your country, she thought but didn't say out loud. She didn't want to interrupt Christa's evil monologue when she was just getting started.

"Jonah taught me what I needed to know about the system. Do you know the places you can get in when you're an FBI agent? Doors open for you and I found the one I needed to get out of this place. Now I just need that knife for my buyer, and I can get out of this city. Or better yet, out of this country."

"Why are you telling me all this?"

"Oh, is it too much information?" Christa practically screamed, then dropped her voice as if talking to herself instead of Sloane. "It probably is too much information. But it doesn't matter. You're going to die anyway."

It was official. Christa was out of her mind. She suddenly realized whether she had the other knife or not Christa was there to kill her.

"Why don't you put that down so we can talk," she suggested, gesturing to the ruby handled blade clutched in Christa's right hand. "We can think about this together and figure out who could have taken the knife out of the evidence locker."

"You're such a filthy liar. You have it or, at least, know where it is. Tell me now!"

"I already told you, I don't know."

"Then you're no use to me anymore."

She knew what was going to happen, but she was still slow to react when Christa lunged for her. She'd never been in a knife fight before but reacted instinctively. She stepped back, blocking Christa's stab with her arm. The knife glanced off her forearm, slicing a thin strip of skin, but most of the blow was Christa's arm hitting Sloane as she swung around behind the other woman. Reaching back, she grabbed Christa by the hair jerking her off balance.

Good thing Christa was wearing those ridiculous heels she liked so much and actually stumbled, because Sloane had no idea what to do next. She backed up, searching for something to use as a weapon, her hand landing on the top of a barstool.

"Lucky shot," Christa said, grunting in anger as she pulled herself to her feet, still gripping the knife in her hand. "It won't happen again. At least I drew first blood."

Christa lunged forward again, and Sloane grabbed the barstool, smashing it between the two of them and knocking the knife from Christa's hand. It spiraled away, sliding across the floor.

For a moment, they both stopped, watching the knife spin. Sloane recovered first, jerking the stool upwards, smashing the hard, flat seat into Christa's face.

The agent's head snapped back, blood pouring from her nose. Instead of reaching up to wipe the blood away, like any sane person would have, Christa screamed like an attacking animal as she launched herself at Sloane. She wrapped her arms around Sloane's body, slamming her to the floor and jumping on top of her. Sloane tried flipping to her back, trying to protect her organs as the other woman hammered a fist into her side.

Twisting, she thrust out a leg, knocking Christa back onto her butt. It was purely luck she'd lasted this long, and she knew it. She really needed to enroll in some self-defense classes if she made it through this alive.

On her hands and knees, Sloane scrambled a few steps before gaining her feet and sprinting toward the knife, knowing it was her only defense against a bigger and better trained opponent. If she could just grab the knife, she thought she might have the upper hand.

Flinging things behind her, she tried to slow Christa down with glasses, liquor bottles and even Cher's doll, Greta, soared through the air, smacking into her attacker's face, trying to get to the knife before her.

As she reached for it, Christa's stupid high heeled foot stomped down on the delicate bones in her hand. She shrieked, pulling her hand back and Christa picked up the knife. She tried to stand, but Christa grabbed her hair with her free hand, holding her in place as she lowered the knife toward Sloane's throat.

"I never knew what he saw in you, you know," Christa hissed, out of breath. "He'd go on and on about the connection the two of you had but I couldn't see it.

You are so annoying. Not my type at all. At least I won't have to deal with the mess every time you call, and he goes running to save you anymore."

She watched the knife move closer. She knew she should close her eyes. She didn't want to watch herself die, but she couldn't make herself do it. There were so many times she should have died already—in the car crash with Michael, in that damn hole in Wisconsin, and even when she'd been possessed by a dark entity in Maine. But each time she'd had someone there to save her.

Jonah.

Just thinking about him made her heart ache. He represented everything that was good in her life and she'd killed him. Stabbed him in the chest. It should have been her. He'd kept her alive so many times but the first time it was her turn to save him, she'd failed.

She closed her eyes, picturing his face in her mind. If she was going to die, she wanted him to be the last thing she thought of. Then she'd be with both Michael and Jonah again.

It was so tempting to just give up. To let go of the pain and fade away but she wasn't ready to let Christa win.

She could hear sirens in the distance getting louder and had a feeling Beckie hadn't listened but had called the police. Only they were going to be too late if she didn't do something to keep herself alive now.

Pulling her head down, she screamed an angry war cry as she ripped her hair out of Christa's grip, grabbing the woman's arm and dragging her to the floor with her. They fell in a jumble of arms and legs and she felt the tip of the knife slice deep into her arm. With her other hand, she wrenched it out of Christa's grasp, scrambling to get away.

Christa growled like a wild animal, diving on Sloane and flipping her over. Her back slammed into the hard-wooden floor and Christa was straddling her waist again. Sloane held the knife between them, the rubies in the handle digging into her hand.

"Don't make me use this," she pleaded, trying to sound brave. She'd already killed one person with the knife and she really didn't want to have to do it again.

"As if you could," Christa snarled, grabbing Sloane's wrist and with a swift twist, Christa held the knife over her once again.

Her eyes widened as she rallied all her strength to push Christa away from her. But Christa was stronger and had more leverage than she did. The blonde leaned her body weight into it, pushing the knife down until it hovered above Sloane's heart.

"I can't wait to finally be rid of you and your stupidity," Christa spat. "If I have to hear one more story about you and Jonah ghost hunting together, I'll scream. I have news for you, though you're going to find out soon enough for yourself—THERE'S NO SUCH THING AS GHOSTS!"

"There…are…ghosts," Sloane grunted out. "And I'm…gonna…haunt you…until…you die…bitch!"

Sloane felt the knife slice through her shirt, tearing the cotton fibers, and even though she heaved with all her might, the tip cut into her skin. Tears leaked from her eyes. She wasn't strong enough to stop Christa and this time Jonah wasn't going to come to her rescue. This was it.

Out of nowhere a two-by-four swung from the side,

knocking across the side of Christa's head so hard the board broke in two. She blinked in surprise as Christa's eyes glazed over and she slumped to the side, unconscious.

Chapter 13

"Katie?" Sloane glanced up at the shorter haired twin. "I thought I told you guys to get out of here?"

"I don't listen well. Plus, that blonde bitch needed to be taken out. What did you do to her anyway?" Katie asked, reaching down to push Christa the rest of the way off Sloane and help her to her feet.

"I'm alive," Sloane replied.

She staggered to one of the tables, collapsing into one of the bench seats.

"Sounds about right. I hate people who hate people who breathe," Katie said vaguely, and Sloane tried to smile. "And I don't like being told what to do. Especially in my own place."

"Thanks for saving me," she said.

"Hey, no biggie. I like when people I like are breathing," Katie replied, picking up half the two-by-four again and eyeing Christa as if she thought she might wake up again and need another whap with the board.

"Were you the one who called that cops?" Sloane said though she really didn't want to deal with them right now.

"Beckie did that," Katie snorted. "They should be here soon."

The back door opened, and Sloane looked up to see a familiar looking man in a black bowler hat walk in.

He wore a long trench coat over a gray designer suit and carried a large briefcase in his gloved hand. He tipped his hat at them, skirting the jumble of tables and chairs Sloane and Christa had knocked around during their fight. Sloane didn't even remember moving them.

He knelt down beside Christa's prone form, touching her neck to check for a pulse.

"She's alive," Katie told him. "I don't hit that hard. I was a basketball player, not softball."

The man nodded as if convinced and flipped open his briefcase. Nestled inside in a foam bed carved to its specific dimensions was the sapphire knife Sloane had last seen at the police station in Las Vegas.

The man in the bowler hat picked up the ruby knife, pulling a crisp white handkerchief from his breast pocket to wipe Sloane's blood from the blade. He grimaced, giving Sloane a sympathetic look before placing the knife in the empty place beside the other knife in his case.

He closed the case, snapping the locks back into place before standing. He scooted around a broken barstool, then pulled a folded piece of paper out of his pocket and sliding it onto the table in front of Sloane.

Tipping his hat again, the man walked to the front door, holding it open as Steph came through.

"Good evening, Gryme. Did she have it?" Steph asked, pausing next to the man.

"It was as you suspected," Gryme said.

"And you'll take care of them as we agreed? These knives shouldn't be allowed to kill again."

"I agree. It is a loss but worth it if these blades are put to rest."

"Thank you. I'll be in contact soon." Steph leaned

forward, kissing the man in the bowler hat on the cheek before he continued out the door, the tiny bell signaling his exit.

Sloane knew the confusion she saw on Katie's face was mirrored on her own.

"Um, what just happened?" Katie asked.

"I have no idea," she admitted.

"That was an associate of mine," Steph said, striding to the booth and taking a seat across from Sloane. "He happened to be at the same convention as you in Las Vegas. He contacted me when he received a message—by carrier pigeon, of all things—stating the knives had been compromised."

The off-key tones of the emergency vehicles got closer and Sloane sighed. She'd have to deal with the police again. Ever since Wisconsin she had an extreme prejudice against police officers that she needed to get over. They were only there to help.

The problem was, lately they seemed to be interrogating her a lot.

"What's with the piece of paper?" Katie asked, gesturing to the piece of paper the man had left.

Sloane unfolded the paper. Typed in what looked like old-fashioned typewriter font was a short note.

Ms. Osborne,

Thank you for aiding me in the recovery of the Twin Blades of Butchery. I was able to recover them from the evidence locker before your 'friend' was able to get there. I will take care of the proper burial of the knives on the opposite banks of reverse flowing rivers. That way they will never harm anyone again. The police will be here soon. Do not mention the knives when questioned. Your compensation will be waiting for you after they are gone. I will be in touch sometime in the near future.

Sincerely,

Sir Benedict Harold Gryme

"He says not to mention the knives to the cops," Sloane said, still looking down that the paper.

"He is a wise man who knows what he's doing," Steph said.

"I'll do what you tell me to do. Are you sure that's wise?" Katie asked.

"I'm not sure, but I feel like it's the right thing to do," Sloane admitted, folding the paper and slipping it into her back pocket. What did he mean her compensation would be waiting for her when the cops left?

"In that case," Katie reached over the counter and grabbed the serrated knife used for cutting fruit for drinks. She smeared some of Sloane's blood on it from the slice on her arm and slid it into Christa's hand, squeezing to make sure her fingertips touched the hilt. "That should take care of it."

"Smart thinking," Sloane said, impressed.

****

The front door jangled again, and two officers decked out in all black with bulletproof vest, helmets, and face coverings entered, their rifles trained on Sloane, Steph and Katie. Sloane put her hands up to show she wasn't armed as did Katie.

"This is my bar. That crazy woman just came in here and started attacking my friend, Sloane. We have no idea why. She tried to kill Sloane and was choking her and sitting on her and stuff, so I hit her with a board and knocked her out. My sister's the one who called the police."

Katie said all of that so quickly even Sloane had trouble following, and she'd been there.

Another man walked in. He was dressed in a suit and tie instead of police gear and pulled out a badge Sloane recognized. She'd seen it many times since Jonah had the same one.

"Is everyone all right?" he asked, motioning for the men in black to lower their weapons.

"We are now," Sloane said.

"Your sister called the police, who we currently have blockading the street in case of an incident. We were called in because of an anonymous tip about a rogue FBI agent who'd gone off the grid," he glanced at Steph and Sloane was sure she saw a quick wink. "It seems the two of you have done our work for us."

"How long ago did she turn?" Sloane couldn't stop herself from asking the question even though she knew she should keep her mouth shut.

"It's really an internal matter but, off the record, Ms. McBride was believed to be double dealing in the middle of an assignment. Her partner suspected her defect and had sacrificed his cover to locate her."

"Jonah was undercover, but then my going there…" She couldn't say it out loud. Everything Christa had made her do to "help" Jonah had really only made things worse. She wanted to pick up the board and whack the girl again. Her hands shook but she tried to keep the agent from noticing. It was hard when blood was seeping from the knife wound and dripping onto the table.

"Why don't we get you out to the ambulance for an evaluation while we take care of statements," the agent said kindly, helping her out of the booth and leading her toward the door.

"I'm fine," she insisted but allowed herself to be led outside.

Sitting in the back of an ambulance as an EMT bandaged the cuts on her arm and the damage the high heel had done to her hand, she watched, vaguely disinterested, as Christa was led from the bar in handcuffs. When she was gone, Katie walked over with the FBI agent.

"The two of you need to stay in town for questioning until this case is closed," he said.

She had expected as much.

"I'll be here," Sloane told him. "I'm sure you already have my number."

The agent half smiled before walking away.

"Beckie says we're not only going to be able to pay off the loan, but we're buying the whole area right out from under that cheesy developer's nose," Katie said. "And we're going to get a good deal too since it seems the real-estate agent was doing some underhanded deeds to buy the land up herself and make a profit selling it to the hotel owner."

Sloane snorted, rolling her eyes. That sounded exactly like the Carolyn she'd come to know.

"We're going to keep the remaining buildings as they are and try to get the whole area on the National Registry for Historic Homes," Katie said. "My sister is huge on saving this area."

"Let me know if you need a legit paranormal real-estate agent for any of the homes," she said with a smile. "If you do, I'm your gal."

"Like you helped our uncle?" Katie asked. "Sounds

like fun."

"You'd think so, wouldn't you?" she said, the glimmer of an idea forming. "Sometimes it's worth it, like today when I helped your family. Sometimes it's a bit scarier and even life threatening."

"Still sounds like fun to me," Katie smiled.

"I thought you might say that," she said, climbing down from the ambulance and pulling out one of her cards. "Keep in touch."

"I will," Katie replied, heading back into the bar.

She leaned her head back, sighing. This had been a long day. She just wanted to go back to that fancy hotel and take a nice, long bath and cry some more. The only problem was Steph had the keys.

"Looking for these?" Steph asked, waving the keys to the tiny hatchback in front of her face. "I'm parked right around the corner. I'm going to stay here and help clean up. Why don't you head back to the hotel?"

"I think you just read my mind," she cracked a smile, then groaned as she stood. Her whole body ached like one big bruise.

"I sometimes do that," Steph replied. "I'll see you tonight. Don't fall asleep in the tub."

Sloane waved her away with a laugh as she went around the corner. She hit the button on the key fob, hearing the car beep as it unlocked and looked up, stopping in her tracks.

Leaning against the bright red car was someone she never thought she'd see again.

He was dressed casually, in jeans and a black sweater, his right arm in a shoulder sling. His brown hair was a mess, blowing in the breeze but his blue eyes sparkled as he smiled.

"Jonah," she breathed, not sure if she was seeing him or his ghost, though ghosts didn't usually wear slings.

"You didn't think you could get rid of me that easy, did you?" he asked.

She ran to him, throwing her arms around him and burying her head in his chest as she cried, her tears soaking into his sweater.

"You'd better not be a ghost. I swear to mercy if you are, I'm going to fucking kill you."

"Careful now," he said, slipping his left arm around her. "I was recently stabbed."

She choked on a laugh, looking up at him.

"How are you alive?" she asked, her voice broken by the sobs she couldn't hold back. He was alive! He was here. She knew it in her heart but still couldn't believe.

"You missed," he said, leaning down to kiss her. "My heart that is."

She closed her eyes, relishing the feel of his lips against hers and breathing him in. He pulled back first, resting his forehead against hers.

"The story is a little different than Christa led you to believe. Xavier works for both sides. He was supposed to help us prove Christa was selling valuables to criminals, but the knives enticed him too much.

"He couldn't resist using me—and you—in his side hustle which happens to be kinky videos of violent love affairs. We used him to get to her because we needed to see who her real buyer was. And it wasn't Xavier."

"I don't understand any of this. How could Xavier be helping you if he did all those horrible things? How could you trust him?"

"I didn't trust him. I never will but that doesn't mean I won't use his connections when I need to. I never expected Christa to get you involved. When you showed up that threw everything out of balance. And I'm sorry for saying I'm glad Michael is dead. You know that's not true."

"I know. I even knew it when you said it, I just wasn't thinking straight."

"Neither of us were but we're together now and that's what matters. In fact, I think it should stay that way."

"What?"

"I'm talking about 'us'. Don't you think it's time there was an us?"

"Us? I thought you didn't have time for an us."

"I've taken a leave of absence," he said. "Priorities, you know. When the woman you love tries to kill you, it makes you reevaluate life goals."

"Really? If that's all it took, I should have stabbed you months ago."

He started to laugh, but grimaced in pain, holding his right elbow with his left hand.

"Don't make me laugh," he said. "Let's get out of here before one of the agents tries to get me to work on the case. Want to walk and find a coffee shop?" He stuck out his good elbow and she slid her hand underneath.

"They don't have coffee here," she said, gesturing to the bar. "But it does have killer slushies."

"I don't think mixing alcohol and the pain killers they have me on is really a good idea."

"Well, then it's the city. We'll walk until we find one," she decided graciously.

They passed out of the now familiar neighborhood, walking side by side until they found a small cafe. Outside the coffee shop, Jonah came to an abrupt halt and gave her a serious look.

"What?" A billion terrible thoughts ran through her head. *I did injure him. He doesn't have long to live. He hates me. This is all a dream.*

Then Jonah Prescott did something she never thought she'd see...he knelt down on one knee in front of her and took her hand.

The palms of her hands went from dry to perspiring in a millisecond. She looked around because people on the street had stopped to stare at them. An older lady held a hand over her mouth and waited, like she did...with bated breath.

"Uh...Jonah?" she stammered.

"Sloane Osborne, I have but one question for you." His earnest eyes gave her a piercing stare. He meant business and she found herself more terrified than she'd been on any ghost hunt. "Will you be my..." he paused and stood up. Leaning forward, he whispered in her ear, "...new partner?"

She let out the breath she'd been holding and wrapped her arms around his neck. "I'd love to! But, wait. Maybe you should be my partner. My profession is far more lucrative than yours," she laughed. The crowd clapped their tearful approval, obviously thinking a wedding was in their future.

Laughing, she planted a wet one on his lips then whispered in his ear, "You had me scared. For a second, I thought you were talking about marriage and, even though I love you, I'm not ready for a wedding."

Jonah gave her a warm embrace and held open the

door of the coffee shop. "Someday, Miss Osborne. Someday." He winked.

A word about the author…

Kat Green is the alias of authors KAT de Falla and Rachel GREEN.

Rachel has always believed in ghosts but saw her first full-body apparition while working at an old movie theatre in college. When she met Kat at a writers' conference she knew she'd met a kindred spirit—not only did they both favor Captain Morgan but they were both sensitive to the hereafter. After bonding over a few sippy treats and ghost-hunting adventures, the alias Kat Green came into being.

Kat de Falla lived in a haunted house for too long. When things really heated up, she had several paranormal teams investigate, but things only got worse. When her mother suggested she contact a shaman, one agreed to come, saying she had been waiting for Kat's call. The home was cleansed and sold. When she paired up with Rachel, the idea of co-writing a book about a paranormal real-estate agent seemed perfect. Sloane Osborne and the Haunts for Sale Series was born.

Find out more at www.hauntsforsale.com

Follow Author Kat Green on Facebook, @hauntsforsale on twitter and Instagram.

Thank you for purchasing
this publication of The Wild Rose Press, Inc.

For questions or more information
contact us at
info@thewildrosepress.com.

The Wild Rose Press, Inc.
www.thewildrosepress.com